# Replacements

## Endless War and the Men Sent to Fight It

Alan Quale

# Replacements

© 2016 Alan Quale
All rights reserved.

I want to thank my son, Brian, who helped copyedit my manuscript and encouraged me to continue writing. I am deeply grateful for his support.

Cover design by BespokeBookCovers.com

Printed in the United States by CreateSpace.

ISBN: 0692553223
ISBN 13: 9780692553220

I dedicate this book to my late mother, Annie, who saved every letter I sent home from Vietnam. She also collected and saved the letters I sent to other family members. The correspondence, found in a shoebox in her home, brought back many memories. Without the letters, I never could have written this book. Most chapters end with a letter to my parents or to other family members.

**re\*place\*ment (noun)**

3. somebody filling a military vacancy

# Introduction

America sent its boys to fight the Vietnam War. Of the 58,193 American soldiers who died in Vietnam, 25,493 were age 20 or younger; they were not old enough to order a beer in a bar in most states. Another 17,998 Americans who died in Vietnam were 21 to 23 years old.

I was one of those sent to Vietnam, and I remember watching the young soldiers approach my tent in Duc Pho. I was the supply sergeant for B Company and would assign them their gear. They walked with a certain swagger, their heads held high. Many looked like they were not long out of high school with their boyish faces. All of them had finished boot camp, were trained for the infantry, and were now in a combat zone. They probably didn't know it at the time, but most of them were replacements for infantrymen who were either killed or wounded.

I issued the young men their weapons and gear and arranged to take them by helicopter to the "field," the area where B Company was on patrol. At the beginning of my tour, there was only an occasional replacement arriving at my tent. But as the war continued, casualties soared when B Company was sent to patrol one of the most dangerous areas of Quang Ngai province. This area was a stronghold of the National Liberation Front, or Viet Cong, and it had been completely abandoned by the Vietnamese army.

As more men in B Company fell dead or wounded, more replacements arrived. It became a never-ending gruesome process. Only then did I realize the futility of the Vietnam War and my own role in this deadly course.

This book is based on my experiences in Vietnam, but the story could be told from any war. The basics of war never change. Soldiers die or are wounded, and they're replaced. Still, there are some distinctions between wars. I believe the Vietnam War is the most misunderstood war in American history. And the most misunderstood soldiers are the men who were sent to fight it.

For me, the Vietnam War ended more than 40 years ago, but in a sense, I've never left Vietnam. The memories remain, and as new wars begin, I compare them to Vietnam. I see no difference between a young American on patrol in a desert in Afghanistan versus a young American making his way through the jungle in Vietnam. In both instances, the infantryman is thousands of miles from home, facing the threat of death in a strange land with a strange culture. And there are always the hard stares from the villagers as the American soldiers pass by on patrol.

In Vietnam, I felt fortunate to be a supply sergeant, knowing my chances of surviving the war were far better than had I remained an infantryman. I was transferred out of the infantry, where I carried a machine gun, and named supply sergeant only two months before our company was sent to Vietnam. I was 23 years old and knew everyone in our unit. After we arrived in Vietnam, many soldiers confided in me, telling the good things and the bad things they had done. Sometimes their stories were uplifting, and sometimes they were shockingly cruel.

My book includes accounts of men who committed unspeakable acts of murder. There is no logic for what they did, but the process leading to their atrocities began the day they stepped foot in Vietnam. They were assigned as infantrymen. Their orders were to continuously search for the Viet Cong. Each infantryman would do this day after day until he was killed, wounded, or completed his tour. This is what America sent its boys to do in Vietnam. And if these young men returned home unscathed, there was no "welcome home" parade. Sometimes there was only scorn.

Despite the atrocities committed by some soldiers in Vietnam, most American infantrymen were not heartless killers. They were decent young men whose lives were interrupted when they were sent to fight a war in a distant land. I'll always remember the many courageous men in B Company who never lost their humanity, even in the midst of so much violence. Somehow they rose above it all.

*Replacements* is my personal story from Vietnam. While writing it, I realized how fortunate I am. There were many other soldiers who also had stories to tell, but they didn't survive. They were suddenly gone, and then they were replaced, and the war continued without them.

# Chapter 1

# Arriving in the Promised Land

The night was hot, and the mosquitoes were hungry, even inside the big military tent. I tossed and turned on my cot and brushed at the mosquitoes. "Cheap-ass army," I mumbled. "Not even a goddamn mosquito net."

I flipped on my side and pulled my poncho liner partly over my head. It was hot and suffocating under the liner, but at least it was a shield against the mosquitoes. I tried to relax, but nothing seemed right; even the air felt spent. Then a soft breeze began flowing through the tent, bringing slightly cooler air. I finally began to nod off.

That's when the siren sounded—a strange, high-pitched wailing noise. There was instant commotion in the darkness around me—muffled voices, boots shuffling on the ground, and metallic clicking sounds.

I sat up on my cot and stared into the dark. A soldier brushed my shoulder as he rushed past.

"What's going on?" I asked. "Is there a fire?"

"Incoming!" he shouted.

I listened as the footsteps seemed to flow out of the

tent, followed by silence. I was suddenly alone, and I didn't know what to do. Then I heard a sharp whistling sound. As I dove to the ground, the explosion shook everything, and a blast of hot air raced through the tent.

The sides of the tent, shredded by shrapnel, were flapping from the concussion.

I stayed facedown, covering the back of my head with my hands. My ears were ringing, but I could still hear men shouting somewhere outside the tent. I didn't dare move.

A second round whistled overhead, followed by another ear-piercing explosion and a bright flash of light. Another blast of air rushed through the tent, the canvas sides still flapping. I heard a cracking noise from one of the tent poles, but I stayed facedown on the ground, frozen.

"Son of a bitch, where do I go?" I asked.

There was no answer—only the ringing in my ears, which was growing louder, adding to my fear. I knew I had to move, get out of the tent, and find the others.

I grabbed my M16 rifle, put on my helmet, and ran. Once outside, I froze. I had never seen a night this dark; the only thing I could make out were dim outlines of nearby tents.

Several more mortars came whistling overhead. I dove to the ground again as explosions ripped through the camp. Frantically, I began crawling forward, sweeping my arms in the darkness, trying to find my way. I crawled until my hands brushed against tent canvas.

"Anyone in there?" I shouted. There was no answer.

"Hey, anyone inside?" I shouted louder. "Where the fuck is everyone?"

Then came another whistling sound, this one somehow different than the others. The explosion was deafening, violently shaking the ground. Chunks of debris, dirt, and mud rained down. I lay unmoving on my stomach, stunned by the explosion. I slowly ran my hand over my backside, searching for any wetness, but there was none. I suddenly gasped for air, not even realizing I had been holding my breath.

Then another whistling sound, followed by an explosion. But this time, the blast sounded more distant. I stayed flat on the ground, listening closely as more mortars continued to fall. Each explosion sounded like it was falling farther away from where I lay.

Maybe the Viet Cong were "walking" their mortars across base camp, away from my position. I shrugged my shoulders, breathing a little easier.

*Maybe I'm okay*, I thought. *No thanks to the assholes in my tent.*

Still, something was nagging me as I lay on the ground. I remembered one of our combat training classes in Hawaii. The instructor said the Viet Cong liked to walk their mortars across a base and then follow their mortar attack with a ground assault. My stomach grew tight, and I felt the sudden urge to stand and run.

*Shit, they're probably crawling through the concertina wire right now. They've heard my cries for help and are hoping to find me.*

I began crawling forward at a frenzied pace. The night was still very dark, with occasional flashes of falling mortars in the distance. I crawled silently until I couldn't stand it any longer.

"Hey! Is anyone here? Where the fuck do I go?"

There was no answer. Now I wondered if I was the only one left in base camp. I shook my head in disgust and continued crawling in the darkness until my helmet banged hard against a sandbag wall.

I flipped onto my back, pulling myself up to a sitting position against the sandbags and raising my M16 to the firing position. Staring into the darkness, I was ready to shoot anything moving toward me. I turned my head to the sandbag wall.

"Hey, is anyone in there?"

No answer. I slowly stood and began moving forward in a crouching position, my M16 at my side.

Moving faster now, almost in a full run, I slammed into another wall. The sudden impact sent me flying backward onto the ground, my M16 flying out of my arms. I began crawling in a circle in the darkness, running my hands over the dirt until I found my rifle. Then I stood and slid my hand up the side of the sandbags. This wall was high; I couldn't feel the top. My mind was racing, trying to remember if I'd seen any large tents or bunkers when we entered the camp that morning.

Then it came to me — there had been a bunker near the center of camp. Our convoy had passed within feet of the fortress-like structure. The bunker had a thick roof with several layers of sandbags. Two guards were sitting on top of the roof, manning a 50-caliber machine gun.

I heard a voice in the darkness: "Get your ass in here, and stop screaming!"

I swung around, facing the voice, and moved forward.

"Stop right there! Put your gun on safety!"

Now I could see a dim outline of the man standing in a doorway.

As I fumbled with my M16, he reached out and grabbed my arm, leading me into the bunker. Once inside, my eyes adjusted to the dull light, and I could see soldiers sitting on the ground against the bunker walls. In the far corner, a small flashlight was turned on, facing the wall, slightly illuminating the drab, green layers of sandbags.

"Name!" the man at the door shouted.

"I am Sergeant Quale from B Company, Fourth Battalion…uh…sir."

"New guy," he sneered. "And the last one to the bunker."

There were laughs as I found a place to sit. I opened my mouth to respond but changed my mind. I lowered myself to the ground, leaned my back against the sandbags, and stared hard at the other men. My anger was growing after being left alone in the tent and forced to find my way through the darkness by myself. It was every man for himself, and I was damn lucky to have found this place.

*No thanks to any of these assholes.*

I could feel my face scowling at three men sitting across from me. I recognized them from my tent. Fortunately, they didn't know what I was thinking — or maybe they did, and they didn't care? There was anonymity in the army, as most soldiers limited themselves to only a few close friends.

Another mortar smashed into the ground outside the bunker, a shattering blast that shook the walls and ground. There was a loud cracking noise in the roof, and dust started to float down. Men shouted at one another, and someone began coughing from the dust. Another soldier shone the flashlight up at the ceiling, which looked intact. Then, strangely, it became quiet again in the bunker. I stared at the others, waiting for someone to say something, but no one spoke. I sat in silence with my thoughts, knowing that if I were still outside, crawling in darkness, I might not have survived.

"You're a lucky son of a bitch," the man standing at the door shouted back at me. He still spoke with a sneering voice, and the other soldiers turned to look at me, but this time there was no laughter as they saw my body tighten and the anger grow on my face.

Another mortar smashed into the ground outside, shaking the bunker. Dust continued drifting down from the ceiling. As I looked up, my right leg began to tremble. I grabbed my leg, not wanting to show my fear to anyone, and began rubbing it, as though I had injured it.

"I tripped on some fucking wire running over here," I said to the man sitting next to me.

He said nothing and only grunted in response.

After a few minutes, my leg stopped shaking, and the ringing in my ears began to fade. Now I could hear distant small-arms fire, probably from the bunkers on the camp perimeter.

Sweat began dripping from my forehead onto my lap. I stared down at my hands, still tightly clutching my M16. As I loosened my grip, my hands began to ache, but a certain calm was slowly settling over me. For the first time, I noticed that the air inside the bunker was hot, with the strong stench of body odor. But none of that mattered; I felt relatively safe inside these thick walls, sheltered from the mortars falling outside. I also was confused, not knowing what to expect next. I had arrived in Vietnam early that morning, part of an advanced landing party for the 11th Brigade. As the supply sergeant, I accompanied my company commander on the long flight from our army base in Hawaii. We separated when we arrived at this camp; I went to an enlisted men's tent, and the commander to the officer's tent. Now I wondered where he was during this attack.

The rifle fire from the perimeter bunkers was growing louder, a strangely comforting sound that seemed to add another layer of protection for all of us.

The attack on the base continued all night long, the rifle fire fluctuating to heavy bursts and then dropping off to individual shots being fired. The mortars continued to fall, but less frequently. Then, at dawn, the battle suddenly stopped, and a strange quiet settled over everything.

The soldiers, huddled on the floor of the bunker, began nudging awake those who had been able to sleep. Soon everyone stood and began filing out the entrance, apparently heading back to their work areas. They all looked tired, like they were used to this routine.

As I followed the group outside, I saw two adjacent tents that had been destroyed, piles of black, smoldering canvas and debris. The other soldiers were unimpressed, stopping only briefly to look at the smoldering ruins. I followed them past the destroyed tents and looked down the hillside.

The base camp, called Landing Zone Bronco, looked different in the morning sun. Walls of green sandbags surrounded the tents that had not been damaged, and sand-colored pathways ran between the tents. The camp was small, with two rows of tents facing the perimeter, where several guard bunkers sat with rows of concertina wire strung in front. On the other side of the concertina wire were the rice paddies. Several Vietnamese farmers had already arrived with their water buffalo to pull small plows between rows of rice. The paddies stretched for several miles to the west, ending at the base of towering mountains covered with thick jungle, a likely refuge for the Viet Cong after their nighttime attack.

It felt good to be out of the bunker, away from the stench inside. A fresh, warm breeze was moving through camp, and in a nearby tree, several large, yellow birds were singing as though nothing unusual had happened. Everything looked so calm and peaceful. It was hard to imagine that the base had been under attack only hours before.

Still, I wondered how many people had been killed or wounded that night. I scanned the rice paddies to see if I could spot any Viet Cong bodies in the water, but there were none. There were only the farmers at work.

I felt safe, at least for the time being. I sensed this was a landmark moment. I had survived my first mortar attack in Vietnam. I smiled slightly as I began walking down the hill toward my tent.

But then I stopped, and my smile vanished. My sense of relief was suddenly gone, vanquished by a single thought: *I survived my first night in Vietnam, but I have so many more nights to go.*

5 December 1967
Duc Pho, Vietnam

Dear Mom and Dad,

Well here we are in the "promised land." If you have a map of Vietnam, you will see that Duc Pho is located south of Da Nang. The name of our base camp is Landing Zone Bronco, but everyone calls it Duc Pho.

I am part of the advanced party for the 11th Brigade, and all of us flew over on the same flight from Honolulu, a 10-hour flight. There are about 100 of us in the advanced party, including all the supply sergeants and company commanders. We'll be setting up a base camp for the brigade before they get here. After landing in Da Nang, we put on our equipment, took our rifles out, and then flew by helicopter down here to Duc Pho. We will only be here in Duc Pho for two days, and then we will move to a new area a few miles out.

The brigade will board a ship in Honolulu tomorrow, it will be a 20-day trip so they won't be here for some time. We're going to be very short of men at our new camp, especially on the perimeter. Needless to say, I'll be glad when the brigade gets here. This area of Vietnam is supposed to be secure, with few VC. Last night, however, was a little hairy for us newcomers. Mortars fell and small-arms fire blasted away almost all night long.

Today a small group from our brigade will do a reconnaissance of the area where we'll be setting up our base camp. Tomorrow we'll all be moving there and getting settled.

Write and let me know what's happening back there in the world.

Your son,
Alan

# Chapter 2

# Marijuana for Sale at the Orphanage

After the nightlong mortar attack, I returned to the enlisted men's tent. I was surprised to see Captain Earl Lewis, our company commander, waiting inside. He was tall and muscular with a square jaw, and his blue eyes penetrated his listeners when he spoke.

"Sergeant Quale, I've got a laundry plan."

"What's your plan, sir?" I asked.

"When the troops arrive here, we're going out to the field, and they're going to get really stinking dirty out there in the jungle. So you need to set up some sort of process to get their fatigues, underwear, and socks cleaned. I'm told some of the companies stationed here have their clothes laundered in Duc Pho. There's no laundromat, of course, but I think the women wash clothes on the rocks down by the river."

"But how am I going to—"

"Go see the supply sergeant at the motor pool," said the captain. He had a habit of cutting off his subordinates in midsentence.

"What's the sergeant's name?"

"I think it's Sanders or something like that," he said.

He turned to leave and then paused for a moment. "The officers have a small bunker up by their tent, and that's where I spent most of the night. Kind of noisy last night, wasn't it?" He was grinning now, as he stood in the doorway. "If we have another mortar attack tonight, keep your ass low to the ground. That's an order."

"Yes sir, I'll do that."

The captain left, and I went to find Sergeant Sanders. I saw a soldier walking nearby, and I stopped to ask directions. He pointed to the north.

"He's over there; you can't miss him," he said.

The base wasn't that big. It was just clusters of tents at the bottom of a large hill, which was covered by brush. The base camp was called Landing Zone Bronco because there was a strip of metal sheets embedded in the ground near the perimeter where helicopters and small planes could land. I walked past the landing strip and followed the dusty trail between tents to the north edge of camp where the trail stopped in front of a large tent. At the front of the tent was a faded wooden sign that read Supply Tent.

When I entered the tent, Sergeant Sanders was sitting behind a table. I was surprised to see his long brown hair and unshaven jaw. Apparently the US Army relaxed its grooming rules in war zones.

Sergeant Sanders was bent over some papers and simultaneously talking on the radio. I waited on the far side of the tent as he continued to speak into the handset, occasionally glancing at me.

"So when will it arrive?" someone asked on the radio.

"It'll be there on the morning chopper," Sergeant Sanders said. "Over and out."

Sanders laid the handset on the table and stood. I stepped forward, and we shook hands. "I'm Quale from B Company, Fourth Battalion, Third Infantry. I'm part of the advanced party for the Eleventh Brigade. They sent us supply sergeants over here early with our company commanders to get things set up. The brigade is coming by boat from Pearl Harbor, and they won't be here for twenty days."

"Lucky you," Sanders said, a grin forming on his face. "I hear you guys are setting up your camp at Carentan, a few miles out."

I nodded, although this was the first time I had heard the name Carentan.

"Keep a sharp eye on the ground out there," Sanders continued. "I'm told the French had a fire base there during their war, and they put their goddamn mines everywhere. There might be booby traps too, so you need to be careful."

"Thanks for the tip," I said. "But the reason I'm here is that the old man wants me to set up a laundry plan for the troops in our company."

Sergeant Sanders stood, grabbed his M16 and motioned for me to follow him. "Come on, I'll show you."

Outside the tent, we approached his jeep. Before climbing in, I stared at the floor of the jeep, which was covered with sandbags. I also noticed the large gas can strapped to the back.

"The sandbags are there in case we drive over a mine, they're supposed to save your ass when the mine blows," explained Sanders, grinning. "And the gas can, that's simple enough. You'll need it if you run out of gas." The grin was fading as Sanders spoke. "Believe me, you don't want to run out of gas and end up stranded alongside Highway 1. That's what happened to supply Sergeant Bowman from D Company two months ago. They found him in the ditch with a bullet in his head."

We climbed into the jeep and drove down a dusty, rutted road leading out of base camp. When we approached the camp gate, a guard motioned for us to stop. He placed his hands on the side of the jeep and leaned forward.

"Where you going?" he asked.

"Duc Pho, for laundry," Sergeant Sanders said.

"Stay alert," the guard said. "We're told the Viet Cong are in town today."

Sanders nodded yes, and we drove off, the jeep bouncing hard on the rough road leading into Duc Pho. The village was a large cluster of thatched huts, closely packed together. A few palm trees rose up between the huts, and animal pens were scattered throughout the village. Highway 1 was the only paved road, slicing through the middle of Duc Pho. In the center of the village, the road widened, and merchant stalls lined the street. There was also a large bunker adjacent to the road, with thick walls made of concrete blocks. "That bunker belongs to the Army of the Republic of South Vietnam," Sanders said. "ARVN for short."

As we continued driving through Duc Pho, a swarm of boys suddenly ran out from the thatched huts, their thin arms reaching into the jeep. "Hey, GI, give me candy!" they shouted.

"Keep your eyes on the little bastards," Sanders said as he slowed the jeep but continued driving forward through the mob. We drove out of the circle of boys and turned onto a side road, which led to a large, plaster-covered building with fading white paint. A low wall surrounded the building, and two small boys stood at the open gate.

"Hey, GIs, want dope?" they shouted as we drove up. "Plenty good stuff."

Sanders stopped the jeep and gave a boy some piastres, the Vietnamese currency. The boy reached into a cloth sack and pulled out what looked like a pack of cigarettes, handing them to Sanders.

"Here," the boy said. "You be plenty happy."'

As Sanders drove up to the building, he showed me the pack of marijuana. "It's really potent and it gives you a nice high," Sanders said. "And it's cheap too. The Viet Cong make sure of that."

"Why would the Viet Cong do that?" I asked.

"They *want* us to get stoned," Sanders said. "If we're stoned, the VC think they can sneak up on us in the middle of the night and slit our throats."

We got out of the jeep and walked toward the building. Two Vietnamese nuns stood in the doorway. The nuns were short in stature (typical for adult Vietnamese), but the long cloths that draped from their heads made them look a little taller. They smiled and bowed slightly.

Sanders greeted them in Vietnamese and bowed. "This is a Catholic orphanage," he said, turning to me. "The orphanage gets no support from the government or anyone else. So the only way the orphanage can survive is to clean the GIs' laundry.

"Sister Ling here will set it up for you," he said, as one of the nuns stepped forward. "All you have to do is bring the dirty laundry and give it to her. She'll get it cleaned in a couple of days, and you can come, pay her, and pick it up."

Sister Ling said something to me in Vietnamese, and I nodded and smiled back. Sanders and I turned and began walking back to our jeep.

"The orphanage also runs a thriving marijuana business," said Sanders, the grin forming again on his face. "They sell the best dope in Duc Pho. You saw the boys at the gate. They're orphans themselves, part of the marijuana sales team."

Sanders looked at me as though he was expecting a response, but when I said nothing, the grin faded from his face. He seemed to sense that I was questioning whether the Catholic orphanage actually sold marijuana.

"Everything I just told you is true," he said in a loud voice. "In Vietnam, you survive any way you can. Believe me, you'll learn that soon enough."

On our way back through Duc Pho, the same group of boys again came rushing out of the huts, mobbing the jeep. Sanders seemed less patient this time and slowed the jeep only slightly. My body tightened as I watched several boys jump out of the way at the last moment, the jeep missing them by inches.

Finally, we drove free of the young mob. I breathed easier and turned to look back at several boys lingering on the street. Two of them had their arms raised above their heads, giving us the finger.

*Future Viet Cong*, I thought.

We followed the dusty road back to camp. As we approached the gate, the guard stepped forward, raising his hand for us to stop.

"Looks like someone stole your gas can," the guard said, motioning to the back of the jeep. We turned to look at the straps that hung free where the gas can once was fastened.

"Son of a bitch," Sanders screamed. "Those fucking kids."

We drove in silence into camp, but Sanders' sour mood seemed to be fading. He said he had one more thing to show me. We drove past the tents and began following a narrow, steep trail that wound up the hill in the middle of camp. At the top, Sanders parked the jeep, and we got out and looked down at the tents and perimeter bunkers that formed a line between the camp and the rice paddies. A quarter mile past the perimeter, to the west, were the tightly clustered huts of Duc Pho, and farther west, the mountains rose up from the rice fields. "Come on," Sanders said, motioning to me. I followed as he walked to the other side of the hilltop.

The view from the opposite side was dominated by the South China Sea, a long blue crescent extending across the horizon. Below us, waves rolled up onto a narrow beach bordered by thick jungle. Concertina wire and bunkers formed an abrupt partition between the jungle and camp. I watched the frothy waves crash onto the white sand and closed my eyes, breathing the warm smell of the ocean. For a moment, it felt like I was back in Hawaii. But I suspected that this beach, even with its tropical allure, was a dangerous place. The Viet Cong could be waiting in the jungle.

We walked back to the other side of the hilltop, but before getting into the jeep, we stared once more at the distant mountains.

"Those mountains extend all the way to Laos," Sergeant Sanders said. "The thick jungle up there provides easy cover for the Viet Cong and North

Vietnamese troops. That's why we'll never win this fucking war, no matter what those dumb shits say in Washington."

I looked down at Landing Zone Bronco again before climbing into the jeep. The base camp looked small, isolated, and vulnerable. Sergeant Sanders said the nearest American base was at Chu Lai, about 50 miles to the north. It was easy to imagine enemy troops rushing down from the mountains and sweeping through Landing Zone Bronco before any help could arrive. We climbed into the jeep and drove down the hill. Sanders dropped me off at my tent, and I got out and thanked him.

"If you need anything, let me know," Sanders said. "And remember, don't get your ass blown away by one of those mines at Carentan."

I went inside the tent and flopped onto my cot. I was tired after little sleep the previous night, but I didn't fall asleep as I lay on the cot. The images of the base camp kept racing through my head. From the hilltop, the camp looked so small and vulnerable. I could see why it was a tempting target for the Viet Cong, and I wondered whether there would be another attack that night.

Something was wrong with the siren that night; it didn't sound, even as the base camp came under attack once again. This new attack was different, though. There were no mortars whistling overhead. Instead, there was one deafening blast at a bunker located a short distance outside the base perimeter. The bunker was ablaze in the middle of the rice paddies, as small-arms fire erupted from the other bunkers.

Everyone in my tent grabbed his rifle, ammunition, and helmet and began filing out. This time, I went with the others. As we stepped out of the tent, we could see flames billowing out of the bunker outside the perimeter.

We began moving up the slope toward the large bunker. Halfway up the slope, I paused with another soldier to look back at the burning bunker.

"That bunker is a listening post," he said. "It's outside the camp perimeter so that those inside the bunker can see or hear Charlie coming before he reaches camp." He saw the confused look on my face. "We often refer to the Viet Cong as Charlie," he explained. "Tonight those guys in that bunker obviously didn't hear Charlie coming, and now they're blown up by those fucking sappers."

"What's a sapper?" I asked.

"It's an asshole VC who mostly carries bags of explosives. At night, he'll crawl through the concertina wire toward camp. If he manages to break through the perimeter, he throws the satchel charges in tents and bunkers, creating as much confusion as possible inside camp, hoping the Americans will start shooting at each other. Then, if the sapper is lucky, he'll make his way back out of camp and through the concertina wire."

Just then, a jeep with a 50-caliber machine gun mounted in the back burst through camp gate, racing on a trail toward the burning bunker. The jeep's machine gun was spraying fire on the area as it approached.

When it reached the burning bunker, two figures jumped out of the jeep and began dragging two bodies away from the flames. We could see them place the bodies in the back of the jeep, and then they jumped in their jeep and raced back to the camp gate.

"Fucking medics are fearless," the soldier told me. "They'll do anything to bring the wounded out."

"Those are medics?" I asked.

"Shit yes," he said, his face turning somber, "But they only took two guys out of the bunker, so that means three guys are dead inside. I know because I've been assigned to that watch before. There are five assigned to that bunker."

He took one last look at the burning bunker and sighed loudly. "Fucking Charlie is going to kill us all if we don't get out of this rathole."

As we entered the bunker, the air inside was hot and smelled of body odor. We took our seats on the floor, waiting for the mortars. A half hour passed, and there was nothing. I was nodding off to sleep when the first mortar struck somewhere outside. The bunker shook, and dust drifted down from the ceiling.

I was beginning to feel a dull monotony in this war. One moment you might feel safe — even bored — and then, in an instant, you might die in a burst of deadly violence.

Just moments before, I stood and watched flames

consume the bunker where three men died. I stared in disbelief at the inferno — it was so close to us. I could smell the smoke. I wasn't sure, but I thought I also smelled the stench of burning flesh.

Even more upsetting was the realization that one day soon — probably very soon — I would be assigned to a bunker just like that one.

6 December 67
Duc Pho, Vietnam

Dear Carol and Wally,

It's hotter than hell this afternoon, but here we are in the booming metropolis of Duc Pho. And when I say booming, I mean exactly that. Last night, we had more mortar, artillery, and small-arms fire blasting away most of the night. I guess the Viet Cong try to break through the camp perimeter here every night.

We arrived here two days ago, but we'll be moving to another camp a few miles out and getting it ready for the brigade, which will get here in about 20 days.

The village of Duc Pho is very near our camp. Most of the buildings in Duc Pho are thatched huts, and most of the people seem to be farmers (and probably Viet Cong at night). The village is mostly off limits to American GIs.

Well, I guess it's the season to be merry, but somehow I can't get in the spirit this year. Instead of wishing me a Merry Christmas 1967, you can wish me a Merry Discharge in August 1968. I'm down to 8 months and 16 days before I get out of the army, so that makes all of this crap a little easier to take.

We really haven't done anything yet, so there's not much for me to write about. After tonight's mortar barrage (I'm, sure there will be another attack), I will *probably have more to write.*

*Scratch me some lines, because mail is supposed to boost a GI's morale (especially us war mongers over here in Vietnam). Let me know what's happening on your side of the world.*

*Alan*

*P.S. I was promoted to sergeant before we left Hawaii.*

# Chapter 3

# Shooting Starts When the Sun Sets

As our convoy followed the road south from Duc Pho, the land seemed to open up. The rice paddies were much larger, and there were fewer hedgerows of palm trees and bushes between the fields. The air was fresher, and I could smell the nearby ocean.

After driving for several miles, we saw a tall hill rising up from the lowlands. The hill stood alone, separated from the distant mountains by an expanse of rice paddies.

As we neared the bottom of the hill, the convoy approached a river, barely distinguishable from the adjacent flooded rice paddies, separated only by a long, thin line of dikes. There were no rice paddies on the other side of the river. There were only the lower slopes of the big hill.

A wooden bridge spanned the river, and a US Army tank was parked on the far side, its large barrel directly facing the bridge and road. The tank crew was sitting on top the tank, waving at the convoy as we rumbled across the bridge.

After passing the tank, the convoy continued past

the hill before turning off the road onto a smaller trail. The trail wound a quarter mile through shoulder-high brush and tall trees before entering a large grassy area. We had arrived at Carentan, which was to be our new base camp.

The trucks and jeeps pulled into a wide circle and slowed to a stop, reminding me of those Western movies where settlers circled their wagons to defend themselves. Here we were, halfway around the world, and our truck convoy was using the same defensive technique in South Vietnam.

The officers were the first to get out of the vehicles and they began barking their commands. I jumped down from the back of a truck and cautiously looked at the ground, remembering Sergeant Sanders' warning about the mines.

"Sergeant Quale, I've got our position marked," Captain Lewis hollered. I looked up to see the captain motioning for me to come to his jeep. He laid a large sheet of paper on the hood of the jeep.

"You're over here," Captain Lewis said, pointing to a small square on the hand-drawn map of Carentan. "This is your supply tent; the ammo bunker is right behind it."

"Why is the ammo bunker behind my tent?" I asked.

"I volunteered you to be the primary sergeant of the guard for the camp perimeter until the brigade arrives," he said. "So you will be handing out the ammunition, grenades, and claymore antipersonnel mines to those assigned to guard duty, including the sergeant in charge. And then on the nights when you're the sergeant of the guard, you'll also be checking the bunkers on the base perimeter, making sure everything is okay."

"Where will you be, sir?" I asked.

"I'm over here in the officers' tent," the captain said, pointing to a larger square on the map. "These are the officers' quarters."

The captain looked directly at me. His penetrating eyes seemed to be reading my thoughts.

"Okay, sir. What do I do first?" I asked.

"Set up your supply tent, and then come down to the officers' quarters and see Captain Mendoza. He'll give you instructions for setting up the perimeter guard for tonight."

"Tonight?" I asked.

"That's right," he said. "I volunteered you, and be careful where you walk around here. I'm told there are lots of mines." I nodded back at him, and he turned to leave.

*Son of a bitch,* I thought. *The old man's volunteered me to be sergeant of the guard on the very first night.*

I turned to the area where my supply tent was supposed to be located and began following a narrow trail though the brush. Soon the trail emerged into a small clearing where three GIs were lifting the poles for a tent on a grassy patch of ground. The canvas was draping from the top of the poles, and I helped them straighten the poles until the tent's roof took shape. They pounded stakes into the ground, anchoring the tent, and then they gathered up their tools to leave.

"There you go, Sarge," one of the GIs said. "The tent is all yours, complete with a shitload of ammunition out back."

I nodded and thanked them and went inside the tent, laying my gear on the ground, except for my M16, which I continued to carry strapped to my shoulder. I stepped outside and walked around to the back of the tent. Several wooden cases of grenades, claymores, and ammunition were stacked on the ground.

I stared at the explosives so close to my tent, wondering what would happen if a mortar landed nearby. I was almost relieved that I had sergeant of the guard duty that night, away from the piles of ammunition.

But then, guard duty might not be any safer, especially checking all the guard posts on the perimeter—and doing it in the dark. Carentan was already beginning to feel like a dangerous place.

At the officers' tent, I found Captain Carlos Mendoza, a tall burly man with brown skin and thick black hair formed in a perfect crew cut.

"Come on," he said. "I'll show you where everything is."

The command tent for Fire Base Carentan was located near the center of camp, at the foot of the hill. Inside the tent, clerks were busy setting up their work areas. Near the door to the tent was a small wooden table, with a radio sitting on the ground next to it.

"You'll be here," Captain Mendoza said, pointing to the table and radio. "There are twelve guard posts on the camp perimeter, and every guard post will have a radio tonight, so that's how you'll communicate with everyone."

He paused to see if I had any questions and then continued. "Of course, we haven't built the bunkers yet, so those assigned to guard duty tonight are out there on the perimeter right now, digging foxholes and filling sandbags. I want you to go out to the perimeter at least once during the night and check each guard post. Make sure the troops are awake and alert. It won't take long for the Viet Cong to learn we're here, and the first thing they'll do is try to break through our perimeter."

"Yes sir," I said.

Several hours later, I arrived at the command tent as the sun was lowering in the west above the mountains. I laid a pad of paper and pencils on the table and decided to make a quick check of the perimeter to see where everything was located. I wanted to see the entire perimeter before nightfall.

Captain Mendoza had given me a rudimentary, hand-drawn map, showing where the guard positions were located surrounding the hill. I left the command tent and started walking down the slope toward Guard Post Number One on the map.

As I approached, I could see two GIs digging a large hole in the ground; a third soldier was filling sandbags with the dirt shoveled out of the foxhole. They stopped working and stared at me, mopping the sweat from their brows.

"I'm the sergeant of the guard tonight," I said. "I'm Quale from B Company. I'll be back later when it's dark to see how things are going. The password tonight is Nancy Sinatra."

One of the GIs looked puzzled. "So what does that mean?"

"You don't know how to use a goddamn password?" I asked.

"I'm a clerk in Headquarters Company," he said. "I usually shuffle papers."

I realized then that our camp was defended not by infantrymen but by men whose army training was far removed from guarding a perimeter. The clerk was staring at me, waiting for my response.

"It means that if someone approaches your position in the dark, and you can't see who they are, you should challenge them by saying, 'Who goes there?' If you challenge me like that, I'll respond by saying 'Nancy Sinatra.' Then you'll know I'm not the Viet Cong coming to kill you."

"Okay, got it," the soldier said.

"You guys are Post Number One. See you later, and remember the password."

"Marilyn Monroe?" someone asked.

"Fuck you," I said as I walked away.

I made a fast hike around the base perimeter, stopping briefly at each guard post to see how the foxholes were shaping up and giving the soldiers the password.

The sun was sliding down behind the mountains when I arrived back at the command tent. I felt better now that I had seen the perimeter.

I went inside the tent and began calling the guard posts on the radio to make sure the communications were working.

"Post Number One, this is Sergeant Quale. Can you read me? Over."

"Loud and clear. Over."

"That's good. Anything to report from your position? Over."

"That's a negative, except for monkeys fucking in the trees."

"Keep it clean!" I barked into the microphone. "You don't know who's listening to this transmission!

Over."

There was silence on the radio for a moment, and then the voice came on again. "Okay. Over."

As I continued calling the other guard posts, my duty as sergeant of the guard was beginning to feel like a routine army task. Everything was quiet on the Carentan perimeter, but still there was that nagging thought. As the night wore on, I knew the time was approaching when I would have to leave the command tent and make my way alone through the darkness to each guard position.

I tried to calm the tight feeling in my stomach, noting that the perimeter was quiet. Maybe it was so quiet that Charlie didn't even know we were here? Still, it was hard to believe the Viet Cong had somehow missed seeing our convoy rumbling down Highway 1.

*Maybe Charlie is scouting our base camp right now from the brush and trees on the perimeter, waiting for the right moment to attack?*

At 0300 (3 a.m.), I finally put on my helmet, grabbed my M16, and walked out of the command tent. As I stepped outside, I was relieved to see a quarter moon lightly illuminating the camp. Walking toward the perimeter, my eyes adjusted to the moonlight, and I began to see shapes — tents, jeeps, and army trucks. I could also see Guard Post Number One. I slowed my pace as I approached, waiting to be challenged, but no one said anything.

"Anyone home?" I shouted.

"Who goes there?" someone called back.

"Nancy Sinatra," I said.

"Well, come on in here, Nancy," someone said in a mocking voice.

I laughed a little as I approached and stared down at the troops in their foxhole, which was quite deep.

"Good job," I said. "Charlie will never see you in there."

I didn't know what else to say, so I turned to leave, but then I remembered our previous conversation on the radio.

"Oh yeah, are the monkeys still fucking?"

"Nope," someone answered.

"I don't like to holler like that on the radio," I said. "But sometimes Major Harmon listens to the radio, and if he hears you talking like that, he'll hang you by your balls. He has no sense of humor."

"Yeah, he's a real asshole," said someone in the foxhole.

I looked down the perimeter to the next post, which was barely visible in the moonlight. "By the way, who are those guys?" I asked. "I stopped earlier and talked to them. Their weapons look new, like they'd just taken them out of the box. Are they new in the country, or what?"

"They're cooks from the mess tent," one of the GIs answered. "Real gung-ho, kick-ass cooks."

"Oh shit," I said. "I think we should all say a prayer tonight."

Someone in the foxhole laughed, but I was only half kidding. I turned and walked toward the cooks' guard post, stopping briefly to talk to them before continuing down the trail that led from one guard post to the next. As I moved forward, I tried to walk as quietly as possible while staying on the trail in the darkness. My eyes were focused on the dim outlines of the trees bordering the perimeter, wondering if there really were monkeys out there. Maybe there were only the Viet Cong, getting ready to make their move.

I felt a shiver run down my back as I slowly made my way through the darkness. Everything around me was quiet and still, the bushes and trees shaded black and gray.

I already hated Vietnam at night. I knew that everything could be dark and still, just like the path I was following at that moment, and then everything could suddenly erupt in a blinding flash of violence. Worst of all, no one could see what was coming.

As I made my way along the trail, however, I began to realize that the enemy wasn't the only one hidden by the darkness. I, too, was camouflaged by the dark, a lone figure moving through the night. Would Charlie be able to see me? The thought brought a slight smile to my lips and I paused to think about it.

For the first time I too felt hidden by the night, wondering why I hadn't thought of that before. I became more confident and began moving a little faster on the trail, still scanning the trees on the perimeter.

*If I can't see the Viet Cong,* I reasoned, *they can't see me.*

"So fuck you, Charlie," I whispered softly.

By the time I completed the loop around base camp, checking all of the guard positions, the nervous tightness in my stomach was gone, replaced by weariness from lack of sleep. As I entered the command tent I glanced at my watch, which showed 0400 (4 a.m.) I sat down at the small table and looked at the cots on the far side of the tent where several clerks were sleeping. I could only imagine how nice it would be to lie down and snooze, maybe for just 10 minutes.

I removed my canteen from my belt and took a long drink of water. I could hear someone snoring on one of the cots in the corner. I took another long drink and got ready to radio the guard posts once again.

But first I glanced down at my green pants and canvas jungle boots. My camouflaged helmet was on the ground, the muzzle of my M16 resting on top of it. At times like this, it was still hard to accept that I was in the army, let alone the sergeant of the guard for a small base camp in Vietnam. I was 23 years old, a recent college graduate dressed in green, carrying a loaded M16, and giving orders to men in foxholes.

Suddenly gunfire erupted. It sounded like it was coming from near Guard Post Number One. I picked up the radio handset.

"Guard Post Number One, is that you firing?" I asked.

"Negative," they responded.

There was a pause on the radio.

"Son of a bitch, we're drawing fire from our backside!" they screamed. "I repeat, fire coming from our backside!"

"What do you mean?" I asked.

"They're shooting at us from your direction!"

Suddenly several rounds whizzed through the tent, one of them hitting a table in the center. "Everyone down," I screamed, as we all laid flat on the ground.

The gunfire grew more intense, with bullets ripping through our tent from all directions, the canvas sides flapping all around us.

"Stay down!" I shouted.

The heavy gunfire continued for several minutes and then stopped. I reached up for the handset to my radio and called Captain Mendoza.

"This is Quale. We've got rounds coming from all directions through our command tent!"

"Roger that," Mendoza radioed back. "I've formed a squad, and we're sweeping through camp, looking for a sniper. Hold your position, and don't fire unless fired upon!"

"Yes sir," I said.

I lifted myself to a crouching position and hollered to the others in the tent. "Stay down! Don't fire unless fired upon. They're looking for a Charlie sniper inside camp!"

My voice sounded high pitched and filled with fear. I cleared my throat to sound more like an army sergeant. "Just stay on the fucking ground!" I shouted in a deeper voice.

Everyone remained frozen in the prone position, facing the walls of the tent with their M16s. The minutes passed slowly before we heard the dull thud of a grenade.

"Stay down!" I hollered.

Several minutes passed until the radio sounded. "Target found," Mendoza radioed. "Target eliminated."

"Roger that," I responded.

I placed the handset on the table and stared at my radio, waiting for more incoming calls, but there were none. An eerie silence had settled over camp. I began calling each of the guard posts to tell them what happened.

The remaining night at Carentan was quiet. Not a single shot was fired anywhere. As dawn approached,

I sat at my table and began calling the guard posts, mostly to keep myself awake.

"Guard Post Number Two. Everything quiet at your position? Over."

"That's affirmative."

The sun was rising as I walked out of the tent. As usual, a surreal calm was settling over camp, despite the gunfire only hours earlier. I saw Captain Mendoza standing with a group of soldiers about 50 yards downhill from the command tent, gathered around some thick brush. As I approached, I saw a hole in the ground in the brush, apparently the entrance to a tunnel. A soldier was using his machete to cut back bushes surrounding the entrance.

"Fucking Charlie was right here in the middle of camp, throwing fire at our backsides," Mendoza said, pointing at the hole in the ground. "We finally spotted his position and dropped a grenade in there. Blew his ass away."

I nodded and turned to leave. Then I saw the Viet Cong sniper's body on the ground, a bloody blanket covering most of him. His shiny, black hair was visible at the top of the blanket, and his feet were sticking out of the bottom. One sandal was still on his foot, and his other sandal lay on the ground.

I stared at the body for a long time, my mind almost empty of any emotion. Maybe I was too tired to be shocked, or maybe the tedium of war was settling over me? I wasn't sure of anything. I was hungry and turned and walked toward the mess tent.

After breakfast, I walked back to my supply tent, thinking I might be able to catch a quick nap. But Captain Lewis was standing outside the tent, staring at the cases of ammunition and explosives.

"Crazy night again, wasn't it?" He was grinning as he spoke; he looked like he was enjoying Vietnam.

"Yes sir," I said. "Who would have thought of a Viet Cong right in the middle of camp?"

The captain nodded.

"Well, we've got civilian workers coming from the village today to help build the bunkers," he said. "So go down to the officers' tent and see Mendoza again. He'll be assigning you some workers."

"Yes sir," I said, trying to hide a yawn.

Captain Lewis left, and a few minutes later, I began walking down the hill. I felt almost numb with fatigue as I moved. It seemed hard to concentrate on anything other than the cot in my tent and how nice it would feel to lie down on it and go to sleep, even for a short nap.

I reached the camp gate just in time to see several army trucks arriving, each filled with Vietnamese civilians. They all wore cone-shaped straw hats, loose-fitting clothing that looked like black pajamas, and sandals. They seemed to range in age from very young to older men and women. The older ones looked very worn, their faces deeply lined with wrinkles.

Captain Mendoza assigned one dozen workers to each supply sergeant. He pulled out his map and showed us where to build the bunkers on the perimeter. We looked down at the map and divided the perimeter bunkers among ourselves. Each supply sergeant would be responsible for building three bunkers, we agreed.

"Okay, let's get these goddamn bunkers built!" the captain bellowed.

I went to a nearby truck and began handing out shovels to some of my workers and bundles of sandbags to others. Then I motioned for them to follow me and began walking to the area where we would build our first bunker on the perimeter.

The workers followed. They were mostly silent, except for a few brief comments to one another in Vietnamese. I had no idea what they were saying. When I paused occasionally and turned to look back at them, most smiled, but some wore permanent scowls on their faces. As we moved forward, I briefly touched my M16 rifle, which felt reassuring as it hung from my shoulder strap.

We arrived at the site for our first bunker on the side of the hill where thick brush and trees bordered the perimeter. A partial sandbag wall already existed on the hillside, apparently leftover from the Indochina War. I decided to incorporate the sandbag wall into the first bunker that we were about to build.

I pointed to the existing wall and said, "Incorporate."

Most of the workers looked puzzled, and a few shook their heads. I realized how ridiculous my command must have sounded to them. However, an older man seemed to understand what I was trying to communicate. He stepped forward and patted the sandbag wall, moved his hand in a sweeping motion, and said something in Vietnamese. The workers nodded in agreement.

Within a few minutes, the workers were busy building the bunker. Many seemed to have done this type of work before, as some began filling sandbags, while others began stacking them for the walls.

I drove stakes in the ground to show where the walls should go and tried to supervise the workers, pausing occasionally to help women workers lift heavier sandbags into place.

The older man began to act like a work foreman, giving directions to his fellow Vietnamese. Occasionally, he would stop and turn to me, saying something in Vietnamese as though he needed my approval. I would smile back and nod my head yes.

After several hours working in the hot sun, the bunker was beginning to take shape, the sandbag walls rising on the hillside. I glanced at my watch and motioned for the workers to stop for lunch. The

Vietnamese sat in groups under the shade of the nearby trees. I noticed that most of them carried a small bag of rice with a piece of dried fish. Nevertheless, I began walking among them, handing each a C ration lunch box. Many bowed their heads in thanks and put the C rations in their travel bags, choosing to eat their rice instead. They would take the C ration home for their families.

One young man pointed to his C ration box and said "baby son" and made a munching noise with his mouth.

I sat apart from the workers while we ate lunch, my M16 still hanging from the strap on my shoulder. After the workers finished eating, several rolled cigarettes and began smoking.

The older man approached me, speaking in Vietnamese, and pointed to the existing sandbag wall. There was a small bulge near the bottom of the wall, and he motioned that he would straighten it. I nodded my head yes.

As the man walked to the bunker, I turned and made my way into the nearby brush, finding a small clearing where I could urinate. Minutes later, I was turning to leave when I heard shouting on the other side of the brush. Suddenly, there was the sound of feet pounding on the ground. The workers were running. I burst through the bushes into the clearing. The workers were gone.

"What the fuck?" I stood alone on the hillside,

alongside the bunker wall, facing the perimeter. I pulled my M16 down from my shoulder, and held it in the firing position.

"Lai day!" I shouted. The words mean "come here," one of the few Vietnamese phrases I remembered from our army training.

"Lai day!" I shouted again.

There was no response as I stood scanning the bushes and trees.

"Lai day!" I shouted again in a louder voice.

There was still no response. The silence was unnerving, and I could feel the fear gripping my body as I lowered myself to a crouching position, my M16 pointing toward the trees. My mind was racing, trying to find a clue as to what was happening.

*Where the fuck are they?*

Then I remembered the bulge in the sandbag wall that the old man was going to straighten.

*Oh fuck...*

I slowly rose from the crouching position, still facing away from the wall. I didn't want to turn to look, but I sensed that something dangerous was immediately behind me. I waited a moment, trying to build my courage, and turned. A grenade was hanging out of the sandbag wall, only a few feet from where I stood. The grenade was half covered by sandbags, and it looked like it could drop to the ground at any moment. On the ground below was a torn, discarded sandbag, apparently the bulge that the worker went to fix.

I stood frozen, staring at the grenade, its green metal reflecting the sun. I shielded my eyes and looked down at my feet, searching for trip wires or string. When I saw there were none, I slowly stepped back, away from the wall. Then I turned, carefully swinging one foot around the other, facing away from the grenade. My whole body began to shake. I wondered what the blast might feel like.

I felt the urge to run, but I tried to calm myself. Sweat was dripping from my face onto my hands, which were clutching my M16. As I slowly moved down the hill, still looking for trip wires, I remembered Sergeant Sanders' warning about the mines and booby traps at Carentan.

*And here I am,* I thought. *Son of a bitch.*

"Stay calm," I whispered to myself. "You've got to stay calm." Still, as I slowly moved away from the grenade, my urge to run was growing even stronger. "Stay calm…stay calm…stay calm…"

I began saying the words in cadence as I moved down the hill, all the while searching the ground for trip wires.

I heard some distant commotion and stopped to look up. There was a group of soldiers standing with Captain Mendoza; they were staring up the hill at me, puzzled by my slow movement.

"Don't come up here!" I shouted. "There's a fucking grenade in the bunker behind me! I think its booby trapped! I'm looking for trip wires."

There was silence for a moment, and then Captain Mendoza and the others began shouting encouragement to me. "You've got it, Quale!" Captain Mendoza bellowed. "Just keep moving real slow, and keep looking for wire on the ground!" The captain and troops looked so distant, it was like they were on the other side of an invisible line—the safe side. I knew I was still on the side of danger.

As I made my way forward, I had fleeting thoughts of my family and friends back home, but mostly, my mind had turned numb with fear. I moved slowly and methodically, continuing my monotonous cadence: "Stay calm…"

Finally, Captain Mendoza and other soldiers were directly in front of me. As I stepped across the invisible line, I looked to my left and saw the Vietnamese workers filing into camp from the trees. Everyone was safe.

I exhaled loudly as Captain Mendoza grabbed my hand and gave it a vigorous shake. "Way to go, Quale!" the captain bellowed.

Minutes later, a soldier from Headquarters Company arrived with a rifle and a huge telescope. He peered into the telescope at the grenade.

"What is it?" Captain Mendoza asked. "Is it a Viet Cong booby trap?"

"I don't know," answered the soldier. "All I can see is a grenade hanging there, and it looks dangerous. I'm going to blow it."

He took careful aim and fired a single shot. The explosion was thunderous, sending a cloud of dust and smoke mushrooming upward. Several of the Vietnamese women began to wail and cry. They'd heard this deadly sound before.

As the smoke began drifting down the hill, I stood transfixed, watching the approaching cloud. I felt relief, but I still tasted the fear. Suddenly, my whole body tightened with anger, I wanted to strike out at something, pummel it into the ground.

Then my right leg started to tremble, just as it did the night when I crawled through the mortar attack. But this time, I felt no shame, and I didn't try to cover it up.

*Fuck it,* I thought. *I don't give a shit.*

I slowly lowered myself to the ground, sitting with my M16 lying across my lap, staring at my trembling leg.

It wasn't supposed to be like this, especially in base camp with our sandbagged bunkers and fortified perimeter. I had been in Vietnam for less than one week, and twice, I came close to dying.

Now I wondered what my odds were for surviving this war. If my first week in Vietnam was a guide as to what was to come, the odds did not look good at all.

December 1967
Carentan, Vietnam

Dear Mom and Dad,

I've got staff duty tonight. I have to sit in the battalion command-post tent and call the bunkers on the radio, go check the guard, etc. It's all part of the honors of being promoted to sergeant.

We're now located at our new base camp about two miles from the initial camp. We're still located close to the ocean (about a half mile away), in the middle of a plain of rice paddies. The plain extends inland a few miles, and then the mountains rise almost vertically. I guess that's where Charlie is located, although he comes down here every night and harasses our perimeter. It's almost like clockwork. When the sun goes down, the shooting starts, and the shooting continues until the sun comes up. During the day, the people go back to work in the rice paddies, and life returns to normal.

For the past week, I've been working around base camp with Vietnamese civilians. The other supply sergeants and I supervise them in building bunkers, putting up tents, etc. It's been quite an experience. Some of the Vietnamese speak a few English words, and I have picked up a little Vietnamese, so we communicate fairly well. Although they are quite a bit smaller in size than Americans, they carry their share of the load, and most are pretty good workers.

I suspect some of the workers might be Viet Cong. I doubt they would try anything, but it still keeps me on my toes. I never leave my weapon when I work with them, but I've noticed that some of the other supply sergeants are already becoming lax, and they'll leave their gun lying on the ground, right in the middle of a group of workers.

This base camp is about as secure as the one we were at previously. About the only action is Charlie harassing our perimeter at night. As long as he doesn't start throwing mortars at us, there's not too much to worry about. Right now, as I write this, there's small-arms fire going on all around base camp, but it's like that every night. They throw a lot of flares up here so that the guys on the perimeter can see if someone is out there.

Well, enough of my war stories. Actually, the army is about the only thing I can write about anymore. How bad is that? I'm down to eight months and eight days, so that makes this whole mess a lot easier to take.

The weather has turned rainy the last couple days, but it's welcome because as soon as the sun comes out again, it gets hot. It's hard to get in the Christmas spirit when you're stationed in Vietnam.

Your son,
Alan

# Chapter 4

# B Company's First Casualty

His name was John Henderson. He was age 20, a farm boy from Wisconsin. He was tall—probably six feet—with blond hair and a slim build. His rank was corporal.

But the most distinguishing thing about Corporal Henderson was that he was a "returnee." He had already served one tour in Vietnam, and now he volunteered to return for a second tour. As far as I knew, this was a rare occurrence in the Vietnam War.

When the troops in the 11th Brigade arrived at Carentan, Henderson was assigned to B Company and sent to my tent to get outfitted. I assigned him his M16, a machete, and other gear.

Henderson gathered up his things and turned to leave.

"I hear you're a returnee," I said.

"That's right," he replied. "I rotated out of Vietnam 14 months ago."

I wasn't sure how much I should probe, but my journalism training from college kept pushing me to ask the next question.

"Why did you volunteer to come back to Vietnam?" I asked.

"I don't know. Maybe I wanted the excitement of being in the country again, chasing Charlie." Henderson had a sly smile on his face. "I've got some scores to settle with Charlie."

"Well, good luck," I said. "You probably already know this, but watch out for mines and booby traps, even here in base camp. I almost tripped one the other day."

Henderson grinned as he turned and walked out of the tent.

Two days later, Henderson was dead, shot in the chest by the Viet Cong.

His fate began when he volunteered to be part of a reconnaissance patrol. The squad consisted of 10 men, and they set out from camp in the late afternoon, carefully making their way through the rice paddies, slowly moving toward the mountains.

The squad soon reached the foothills and began a slow ascent through thick, waist-high grass. As they approached a thicket of trees, the squad suddenly came under fire. The men dropped to the ground and returned a heavy barrage of gunfire. Then the shooting stopped. Squad members lay motionless in the grass, waiting for a command from their squad leader, but he motioned for them to remain in place. After several minutes of silence, Henderson crawled through the grass, moving to the side of the squad leader. "If you want, I'll go forward and try to flush them out," he told the squad leader. "When Charlie starts firing, you can see where they are."

The squad leader quickly gave his approval. After

all, he reasoned, Henderson was a seasoned Vietnam fighter and knew what he was doing. "Okay, go ahead," he agreed. "But be careful. We don't know how many of them there are."

Henderson nodded his head and began crawling through the grass toward the tree line. The other men in the squad remained crouched in the grass, occasionally raising their heads to look toward the trees, trying to follow Henderson's movement. They could see the grass bending as Henderson crawled forward, but they soon lost track of him. The grass was perfectly still, Henderson must have made his way into the trees.

Minutes passed before there was a burst of gunfire. Smoke from the gunshots began drifting out of the trees, and then there was a scream. Squad members waited for their next move, but the squad leader motioned for them to remain still. They wondered whether Henderson found and killed the Viet Cong. Was Henderson waiting for the squad to come forward and join him?

Several minutes passed, and the squad leader finally gave the order to move forward. The men began crawling through the grass. As they entered the trees, there was no sign of the Viet Cong, and soon they came to a clearing.

Henderson lay dead on the ground, a bullet wound in his chest. When they moved closer, they saw that his left ear had been cut off, the blood still dripping onto the grass. The Viet Cong had drawn Henderson into their trap and killed him, a precise operation using a minimum of firepower, allowing them to save their scarce ammunition for future battles. The Viet Cong were likely retreating to the mountains, taking Henderson's ear with them as a trophy or perhaps proof of what they'd done.

The squad leader radioed base camp for a liftoff but was told it was too late in the day. The helicopter would come in the morning to retrieve Henderson's body.

"Son of a bitch, we're going to have to wait here until morning," he said. Several squad members groaned as they spread out, forming a large circle around Henderson's, body, which they covered with a poncho.

They spent a sleepless night there before the helicopter arrived the next morning, landing in the grassy area. They loaded Henderson's body on the helicopter, and it lifted off, leaving the squad on the ground. The squad would return to camp on foot.

*** 

Specialist Sam Harris, the newly arrived company clerk, and I agreed to split the duties of the company graves registration officer. Harris would officially identify those killed and assemble the paperwork. I would inventory their personal items and send them home to their family.

Harris went to the temporary morgue, a large tent that had several air-conditioned vaults, and identified Henderson's body.

I gathered Henderson's personal belongings and began inventorying them:

One billfold, brown leather, containing 10 piastres and one five-dollar (US) bill

One silver watch (Timex brand)

Two photos of a female ("Beverly" written on the backs of the photos)

One silver cigarette lighter (Zippo brand)

A packet of six letters

One silver necklace with a silver cross attached

One silver fingernail clipper

One pocket knife, three inches long (brown in color)

I placed Henderson's personal belongings into a large envelope, along with a copy of the inventory list, and sealed it. I stared at the envelope for a long time, wondering what Henderson's family would think when they opened it. I pictured grieving parents and family members—and maybe a girl named Beverly—gathered around the kitchen table.

It was a sad thought, and I felt like I was intruding someplace I shouldn't be. I laid the envelope on the table, walked out of the supply tent, and lit a cigarette. As I stood exhaling smoke into the warm air, I wondered what other tragedies might fall on B Company. We were new in country, fresh from our jungle training in the Koolau Mountains in Hawaii, but now we were in a real war zone, and we would be tested.

I had no idea of what was to come—none of us did. Henderson's death was the first casualty in B

Company, a seemingly isolated killing in a thicket of trees in the foothills near Carentan. We didn't know that more men from B Company would soon be killed. Henderson's death would be the first of many.

But ignorance is bliss, and in the days that followed the killing of Henderson, we continued on with our army duties, trying not to think too much about Henderson's final moments, wondering whether he was still alive when they cut off his ear.

There was something else that bothered me. What if several more soldiers fell dead or wounded? How would B Company operate then? As the company supply sergeant, I should have known these things, but I hadn't given it much thought.

But like so many things in war, the answer would come quickly. The death of Corporal Henderson had already triggered a process within the military bureaucracy. Several days later, a young man arrived at Harris' tent with his assignment orders. Harris completed the paperwork and directed the man to my tent. I assigned him his M16 and gear. The newly arrived soldier became B Company's first replacement.

*Alan Quale*

*Christmas morning 1967*
*Carentan, Vietnam*

*Dear Carol and Wally,*

*Season's greetings! We've got the day off here, but it doesn't mean much as I still have to supply the company.*

*I guess there's supposed to be a truce in the war—it was supposed to go from 6 p.m. yesterday to 6 p.m. tonight. I think the VC did observe the ceasefire last night, because it was quiet all night long.*

*However, the night before was probably the most active since we've been here. A member of a recon squad from our company was shot and killed, and a man from D Company was wounded on the base perimeter. Quite a few VC were also killed around the perimeter, but by dawn, the Viet Cong had pulled most of the bodies back into the jungle. I guess they do that so that their losses don't look so bad.*

*I'm down to seven months and 21 days until I get out of this hole. It seems like a long time.*

*I saw a couple of buddies yesterday who just arrived at camp. One of them is with a helicopter company, and the other is in a brigade headquarters attachment.*

*They both stopped by my tent, and since I'm a good supply sergeant, I gave them both a beer, sort of as a Christmas gift.*

*Most of the troops here are more worried about me delivering their beer rations than they are about me delivering their ammunition.*

*Write,*

*Alan*

# Chapter 5

# Don't Worry — I'm in Base Camp

Once the 11h Brigade arrived in Vietnam, everything changed. The advanced landing party became history, and its members were folded back into the brigade.

In a way, I wished it had never happened. I missed the small-camp environment where everyone knew everyone else. Of course, there were inherent dangers, including cooks standing guard on our understaffed perimeter. But we had survived.

When the full brigade arrived, the camp environment changed completely. Soldiers were loaded onto helicopters and flown into the nearby jungle to search for Charlie. Other units headed out in truck convoys to search villages. The 11h Brigade, the so-called "Jungle Warriors" because of our special training in Hawaii, was assigned to pacify the most dangerous areas of Quang Ngai province.

The 11h Brigade commander was Colonel Marvin Binder. The colonel's hair was gray, his thin face was hardened by years of army service, he never smiled, and he seldom fraternized with other officers. Colonel Binder had been passed over several times in his hope to be promoted to general. So when Colonel Binder arrived in Vietnam, he saw it as the perfect opportunity to prove himself and finally reach the rank of general. The best way to be promoted in Vietnam, the colonel reasoned, was to log the largest number of enemy "kills" in the region.

So each morning, Colonel Binder boarded his helicopter and ordered the pilots to fly over the nearby countryside to search for Viet Cong or North Vietnamese troops. If the colonel saw enemy troops below, he loaded his M16 and began firing.

And when the Vietnamese lay dead on the ground, the colonel counted them as "kills" in his notebook, which he always carried in his pocket. As more of the enemy died, Colonel Binder believed the army would finally reward him with his long-awaited promotion to general.

Perhaps because of his long wait to be promoted, Colonel Binder was also a very suspicious man. He didn't seem to trust anyone. Detached from those around him, the colonel focused on a single goal: removing the colonel insignia from his uniform and pinning the general star in its place.

He continued his early-morning flights in his helicopter. But as the weeks passed by, the colonel realized that his actions might not be enough. He needed more enemy kills to impress the army brass. Colonel Binder began sending his men on patrols into hostile areas were there reportedly were large numbers of Viet Cong and North Vietnamese troops. The number of enemy killed began to climb, but so did American casualties. Under these circumstances, some army commanders might pull their troops back. But Colonel Binder ordered his men to press forward and kill more of the enemy.

It didn't take long for the infantrymen in the field to realize what was happening. They cursed when the colonel's helicopter swooped down, landing near their position. The unsmiling colonel would jump out and bark his orders at the officers. "We need more enemy killed!"

After giving his orders, Colonel Binder would climb back into his helicopter. As the craft lifted off, the colonel would stare down at his men. Within a few weeks, more than a dozen infantrymen fell dead or wounded, and many blamed the colonel for the casualties.

Meanwhile, the colonel chose B Company to conduct the brigade's first search-and-destroy mission in the highlands. The company would be taken by helicopter to a remote area in the mountains where they would make a sweep through several villages. The colonel hoped B Company would find many Viet Cong in the area. He gave strict orders to Captain Lewis to keep a complete log of enemy kills.

There were no words of encouragement from the colonel, there was only the hard stare on the colonel's face as he watched his men board the helicopters, which lifted off and flew west toward the highlands. As the helicopters disappeared over the foothills, I stood alone on the grassy area in the middle of Carentan.

I was still in charge of the perimeter bunkers, so I would pull that watch every third night, but hopefully I could finally get some sleep the other two nights. I not only missed sleep but I missed basic pleasures, such as taking a shower, which I had not done since leaving Hawaii weeks earlier.

I looked at my watch; the resupply requests would not be radioed into camp for three more hours. I grabbed a bar of soap, a towel, and my M16, and I jumped into the supply jeep.

I drove out of Carentan onto the road leading to the river. I was glad to see the tank still positioned at the bridge, and I pulled up alongside it, parked my jeep, and jumped out.

The armor crew was sitting on top of the tank, staring down at me, but they said nothing. I took off my shirt, laying it on the jeep seat so that they could see my sergeant stripes.

"I'm going for a swim in the river!" I shouted.

I walked along the bank until I spotted a trail leading through the tall green reeds into the water. *Perfect*, I thought, as I laid my M16 on the ground, kicked off my boots, and took off my clothes. I followed the trail through the reeds and waded into the water, carrying only the bar of soap. I plunged headfirst into the river, which was cool and refreshing, and there was only a slight current.

I floated on my back and lathered up my body. Then I rolled onto my stomach and dove under the surface, rubbing my hands over my body in a scrubbing motion. It was the most refreshing moment I had experienced since arriving in Vietnam. I rose back up to the surface and floated leisurely on my back, staring up at the dark blue sky, the current slowly carrying me downriver. Then I turned onto my stomach and started swimming back upriver. I could see the tank ahead on the bank, and an army truck was rumbling across the bridge. After several minutes of leisurely swimming upstream, I spotted the trail leading to the bank. I swam until my feet touched the bottom and then began following the tail through the reeds.

At first glance, I didn't see the snake; I almost stepped on it. It had diamond-shaped designs, brown and olive in color, naturally camouflaged as it lay motionless in the reeds. My right foot froze only inches above the snake, and I slowly pulled my leg back. The snake stretched across the path into the reeds, and I couldn't see its head or tail, but its body was as wide as a soup can.

*Holy shit.*

I turned and plunged back into the river and began swimming downstream. As I watched the riverbank slowly pass by, I wondered what else was in the water. Then I began focusing on getting out of the river. I looked to riverbank, where the reeds seemed to be growing thicker and higher. I was starting to panic, knowing that I had to find a place to make my way to the shore.

I soon spotted an area where the reeds thinned out and swam toward it. As I neared the bank, my feet touched the bottom and I began thrashing forward through the waist-deep water. Then, as the water became shallower, I broke into a run to the bank. I stood on the dry land, relieved, breathing heavily and shaking my head. It seemed as though nothing was safe in Vietnam, not even swimming in the river.

I walked upstream to where I left my clothes, pulled on my pants and boots, and picked up my M16. As I walked toward my jeep, I stopped and glanced at the trail through the reeds, but the snake was gone. When I reached the jeep, I laid my M16 on the seat and looked up at the tank crew. "There's a big snake in the river," I told them. "He's in the reeds down there. Scared the shit out of me!"

The men on the tank grinned, and one man started to laugh.

"That's Bertha," he said. "She's always hanging around down there. But we don't bother her; she keeps the rat population down around here."

"Well, you could have told me about her," I said. "I almost stepped on her, for Christ's sake!" I could feel my face tighten, a scowl forming. Then I looked at my watch and saw that it was almost time for the resupply requests to be radioed into base camp.

I jumped into the jeep, started it, and pushed the pedal to the floor, raising a thick cloud of dust drifting back toward the tank. The jeep's tires continued spinning through the dirt until I pulled up onto the road. As I drove toward Carentan, I looked back and saw a thick cloud of dust almost hiding the tank. The scowl was fading from my face when I reached the side of hill and turned into camp.

Not long after I arrived at the supply tent, the supply requests were radioed in from B Company. "One case of mosquito repellant, C rations for 110, 80 sodas, 140 beers..."

The refreshments were the most important item on most resupply lists. Captain Lewis had made that clear to me when we first arrived in Vietnam. "Quale, I want you to deliver either two sodas or two beers to every member of the company every day," the captain said. "It's their choice to make—either they want two sodas or two beers, or they can have one beer and one soda."

Once the supply requests were received, I loaded the supplies into the jeep and drove to the helicopter landing area. When I was done loading everything onto the helicopter, I motioned to the pilots to lift off. I stood and watched the helicopter steadily rise until it banked to the right and headed for the highlands.

I went to the mess tent and ate dinner. On this night, I had no guard duty, so after eating, I walked back to my tent, lit a cigarette, and found my flashlight. When I finished smoking, I turned on my flashlight and lay on my cot, positioning it so that I could read a book in the growing darkness. After reading for an hour, I became drowsy, so I removed my boots and set them on the ground next to my cot. Then I placed my helmet next to my boots and laid my loaded M16 across the toes of my boots with a bandolier of ammunition on top of the rifle.

I was all set for the night. If Charlie attacked in the coming hours, I would swing my legs off the cot and into my boots, simultaneously grabbing my helmet, rifle, and ammunition. I would do this in one swift motion, ready in an instant. I looked down at my gear and smiled at how organized everything looked. It was growing darker, but I would know exactly where everything was located.

I didn't realize it at the time, but I was establishing a routine that I would repeat every night thereafter until my Vietnam tour ended.

On this night, base camp was unusually quiet. I lay on the cot and stared up through the open flap at the top of my tent. I could see stars, but they looked different than the ones I remembered seeing back in North Dakota.

Nothing was the same in Vietnam. Everything looked different.

5 January 1968
Carentan, Vietnam

Dear Claire and Edwin,

I'm sitting here writing this letter on a table covered with malaria pill bottles, heat tablets (for C rations), and other supply items that I'll be sending out to the troops tomorrow.

Today was the first "slack day" I've had since the brigade arrived. Our company went out to hunt for Charlie yesterday (via helicopter). They'll be gone five days. All I have to do now is wait for supply requests on the radio, and then I go down to the landing strip and load the supplies on the helicopter, which takes the supplies out to the jungle. Being a supply sergeant definitely has its good points.

Our company had another casualty last night. A soldier fired a grenade at a bunker with a grenade launcher, and some shrapnel bounced back and wounded him. He's in pretty good shape, though, and it won't be long before he's back in action.

Actually, since the brigade began patrolling this area, we have encountered little action. They did kill five VC three days ago, and they captured two. One of them was a woman. I guess the VC will let anyone fight on their side.

Well, as news is scarce here (unless you like war stories),

*I'd better sign off and do some work on my supply records.*

*Actually, concerning the war, the one thing that bothers me is what the folks are thinking (mainly Dad). I sense from his letters that he's worrying a lot, and I know that's not good for his ulcers. Of course, no matter what kind of letter I write, he's still probably going to worry about me. So please try to keep him calm, and keep telling him everything will be okay. And if he asks whether you've heard from me lately, tell him you have, even if you haven't. That will be our little secret.*

*Alan*

# Chapter 6

# Back to Duc Pho

We soon learned that nothing is stationary in Vietnam. After only a few weeks at Carentan, the order came for the 11th Brigade to move to Landing Zone Bronco.

So we took down our tents, packed our gear and prepared to head back by truck convoy. As I walked to the trucks, I glanced at the first bunker I built with the Vietnamese workers only weeks earlier. In my mind, I could still see the grenade hanging on the wall and my slow, agonizing walk to safety.

We climbed into the backs of the army trucks, and the convoy moved out of Carentan, turning onto the main road. As the convoy crossed the river, I noticed that the tank was gone. I instinctively looked down at the reeds on the riverbank, but I couldn't see any snake. Bertha was also gone.

As the convoy moved north toward Duc Pho, the land seemed to close in again. The rice fields became smaller, and there were more hedgerows between the fields. By the time the convoy passed through Duc Pho, the air was hot, humid, and almost putrid to smell.

The convoy pulled off Highway 1 and bounced down a smaller road leading to the gate of Landing Zone Bronco. The convoy passed through the gate, continued to the northern edge of camp, and stopped next to the perimeter. This would be our new home. When I jumped out of the truck, I noticed that several stakes had been driven into the dirt, each with a sheet of paper stapled to the top.

I soon found the stake with "B Company Supply" written on the stapled sheet. I examined the tent site and looked toward the perimeter. My supply tent site was only 40 yards away from the nearest guard bunker. Farther down the perimeter, a large wooden structure rose next to another bunker. There were no windows in the tall walls, and guard towers were perched on top of the walls.

We soon learned this was the prisoner of war compound. The structure was imposing, with concertina wire stretched on top of the walls between the guard posts. I wondered how hot it must be behind those tall walls, and I wondered what sort of interrogation might go be going on inside, hidden from our view.

Beyond the POW compound, a large tent sat directly on the perimeter. Curiously, there were no sandbags surrounding the tent. I could see men walking naked toward the tent, each carrying what appeared to be a towel. We soon learned this was a shower tent, with pumps bringing water from nearby rice paddies. The water was funneled into hoses that sprayed down onto a wooden floor with spaces between planks to drain off the water back to the paddies.

In the days that followed, we raised our tents and began filling sandbags to surround them. The weather was hot and humid and we sweat continuously as we worked. But near the end of each day, we would throw off our clothes and walk to the shower tent, a refreshing end to another searing day.

After a couple of weeks, our tents were complete and functioning as supply units. All of the supply tents stretched in a straight line, with a narrow path in front. The company clerks' tents stretched in a similar line on the other side of the pathway. It was the typical army layout, even here in a small, remote base in Vietnam.

Soon I learned that I was no longer the sergeant of the guard for the entire camp perimeter. Instead, I would be responsible for only three bunkers on the perimeter below my tent. I would draw up the guard roster each day from the B Company support staff that was stationed in base camp. There were usually about 12 of us in camp, so every man had guard duty every third night. I always included myself on the roster. I knew that if I didn't do this, I would be very unpopular.

Everyone hated guard duty, and soldiers often

complained to me when I assigned them to the roster. I remember Private Luke Santini complaining more than anyone else.

"I just pulled guard duty on Sunday," Santini protested.

"I know, but it's time for you to do it again," I said.

"But I've got a bitch of a job to do Wednesday, stringing concertina wire in that swamp along the perimeter. I've got to stay awake, man, keep my eyes open for creepy crawlies in the water."

"That doesn't mean shit to me. You've still got guard duty tonight," I said. "It's your turn."

Of course, always lingering in the back of everyone's mind was the danger factor; you could die on bunker duty.

However, I always reminded the bunker guards that you could die anywhere in a place like Vietnam. At least the bunkers had sandbag walls and layers of sandbags on top of the roof.

Danger existed everywhere in Vietnam, although it was never spread evenly among the troops. I saw this inequity almost every day, mostly because of my job traveling between base camp and the field.

Base camp usually looked safe. But the villages and countryside where our company patrolled looked forbidding and dangerous. It didn't take long for infantrymen to see this disparity, and I sensed the growing animosity.

"You guys in base camp are all REMFs," a grinning soldier told me one afternoon in the field. I had brought supplies to the company by helicopter, and the soldier was helping me unload.

"We're what?" I asked.

"REMFs," he said.

"What's that?" I asked.

"Rear-echelon motherfuckers," he said.

While danger was often present in the field, everything was far different in base camp. The troops in base camp were there not to fight but to provide support for the infantry. Camp personnel included the company clerks, supply sergeants, weapons personnel, radio repairmen, cooks, medics, and others, all providing some kind of support.

Still, there were times when life in base camp could also be dangerous. For me, one of those moments occurred one month after arriving in Vietnam. I had assigned myself to guard duty, and as I walked down the hill to my assigned bunker, I saw the ruins of the bunker beyond the perimeter that had been destroyed weeks earlier.

When I neared the perimeter I saw Brian Taylor and Chuck Davis standing outside our bunker, smoking cigarettes. I assigned the two of them to the bunker with me because I knew they were dependable, unlike many base camp soldiers. Choosing who would be with you in the bunker was one of the few advantages of being the sergeant who made the assignments.

The three of us went inside the bunker while the sun was still hanging above the horizon. We began the customary search for explosives, since most bunkers were left vacant during the daylight hours. You never knew who might sneak through the concertina wire and place a booby trap somewhere.

Next we searched the crevices between the sandbags, looking for scorpions and centipedes. Both were poisonous, and even a "pinch" from the centipede would make you sick to your stomach. No one wanted to be sick on guard duty.

Once we determined the bunker was safe, we went outside to set up our defenses. I always set up three claymore antipersonnel mines, each about 20 yards in front of the bunker. Then I ran a line from the claymore to the firing device inside the bunker. We also set up an M60 machine gun and canisters of ammo outside the bunker next to a low wall of sandbags. If our bunker came under attack during the night, one of us would crawl outside to man the machine gun, giving us extra firepower.

The nearest bunker to us on our right was 80 yards away. On our left, the next bunker was 100 yards away. All of the bunkers on the perimeter were part of the camp's central defense and controlled by a command center on top of the hill.

Still, the guards in each bunker knew they had a single

mission: to stop the Viet Cong from overrunning *their* bunker. If a neighboring bunker came under attack and faced being overrun, we couldn't leave our assigned bunker and come to our neighbors' aid. That would place our own position in jeopardy.

As a result, we felt somewhat isolated and separated from the other bunkers, even though each bunker was part of the base defense. In a sense, every bunker was fighting for itself, but in so doing, each bunker was also protecting the entire camp from the enemy.

As the sun began to set, we went inside the bunker and looked through the narrow window in the front, scanning the rice paddies and looking for any movement.

It was always hot inside the bunkers. The sandbags were baked all day by the boiling tropical sun, and when the sun set, the sandbags began radiating the heat. The radiation continued all night long, making the insides of the bunkers sweltering hot. On most nights, everyone inside the bunker was wet with perspiration within an hour of sundown.

"Son of a bitch, it's hot in here," Taylor complained as we gazed out the window, looking at the darkening landscape. "It must be 100 degrees in here, for Christ's sake."

"Okay, who wants to do the first watch?" I asked.

"I'll do it," Davis said. "It's too hot to sleep anyway."

Taylor agreed to take the second watch, which left me with the third watch.

"I don't think any of us is going to get much sleep tonight," I said. I walked out the back door of the bunker, hoping to get a breath of fresh air. But the air outside was also warm and murky. Clouds spilled down from the nearby mountains, as the sun began to set. With the thickening clouds, it was going to be a very dark night. I stood outside the bunker, listening for strange noises, but there were none. Everything around us was quiet on this steamy night in Landing Zone Bronco.

I went back inside the bunker, spread my poncho on some sandbags, and laid down to rest, hoping I might be able to sleep a bit. Soon I began to nod off, even as the rivets of sweat dropped down from my hair onto my neck.

Then I awakened to gunfire.

"Son of a bitch," Davis screamed as he dove to the floor. Gunfire was coming through the window of our bunker.

"Holy fuck, they're close," Davis shouted. "Right out front!"

"We can't stay down," I shouted. "Return fire!"

I stood and pointed my M16 out the window, spraying the area in front of our bunker. Then I ducked down.

Taylor loaded his M16, held it above his head, facing out the window, and fired off an entire clip, swaying the barrel from left to right.

The Viet Cong answered with another burst of gunfire. Bullets were ripping open sandbags and sending chips of wood flying from the big wooden pole in the middle of the bunker.

"Son of a bitch!" Davis shouted as he spit some wood chips from his mouth.

"Keep firing back!" I shouted.

We all stood and fired our M16s out the window. Then we ducked down.

"I'm blowing a claymore," I said. "Stay down!"

I found the wire to the claymore and detonated it. The explosion shook the bunker, and soon, dirt and mud began falling on the bunker and splashing into the rice paddies.

"Take that, you sons of bitches!" I shouted.

Everything stayed quiet for a minute, and then the Viet Cong opened fire again, the bullets coming through the window and slamming into the bunker walls.

I stood at the side of the window and looked out, but the night was so dark that I couldn't see any movement. Then I glanced toward the adjacent bunkers, which apparently were not under attack.

"Charlie is zeroing in on us," I shouted. "I'm going outside to blow a flare. Then maybe you can see them."

Taylor and Davis nodded okay.

I grabbed the long, metal tube and went out the back

door of the bunker. The gunfire had almost stopped, with only an occasional round passing overhead. I dropped to the ground and crawled along a low sandbag wall for 30 feet and stopped.

While lying on the ground, I took the cap off the flare, placed it on the bottom, pointed the tube up and slammed the bottom of the tube down hard onto the palm of my hand. This routine was supposed to launch the flare, but nothing happened.

"Son of a bitch, fucking flare," I muttered. I lifted the tube again, slamming the flare down harder on my palm, but nothing happened. "Son of a bitch!"

I was crawling back toward our bunker when my hand felt a hard spot on the ground, a large flat rock. Perfect, I thought. I lifted the tube again and brought it down hard on the rock. The flare shot up and suddenly veered to the left, flying horizontal into the side of our bunker. The flare bounced off the bunker, landing only 10 feet from me.

Now I was illuminated, and the Viet Cong started shooting at me. As I ran toward the bunker, I heard the sizzling sounds of passing bullets, one very close to my ear. I dove forward at the rear of the bunker, landing at the doorway, and crawled inside, my heart pounding.

"Now we're in deep shit," I shouted. "That flare is going to stay lit for another minute. We've got to hit them with everything!"

I found the wire to the second claymore and pushed

the switch. The explosion shook our bunker, and mud and dirt began falling onto the roof.

Davis and Taylor both stood at the window, firing their M16s, while I found the grenade launcher and loaded it.

"Take cover!" I shouted as I pointed the barrel of the grenade launcher out the window. I pulled the trigger, and moments later, there was a bright flash as the grenade exploded out front.

"Again!" I shouted as I loaded a second grenade. We all ducked down as I fired the second round.

We stopped shooting and listened. It was quiet for a moment, and then the Viet Cong opened fire again.

"Son of a bitch! We've got to hit them with the machine gun," I hollered.

"I'll do it," Taylor volunteered.

"Stay down, below the sandbag wall," I said. "Just keep firing."

As Taylor crawled toward the machine gun, I blew our third claymore. This time, the explosion was much louder, a deafening sound.

"I saved the best for last," I said, grinning at Davis. But Davis wasn't laughing. I could see the fear on his face, even in the darkness, and I felt the same fear in my gut.

The field phone rang on the pole on the middle of the bunker. I brushed splinters off the handset, surprised that it still worked.

"Bunker seven, Quale here!"

"This is Sergeant Trujillo from command on the hill. What are you guys firing at down there?"

"We've got VC out front!" I shouted.

"Hold your fire, for Christ's sake!"

"Did you hear me?" I shouted. "We've got VC out front! We're not holding our fire, you shithead!"

Suddenly the phone went dead, and I dropped the receiver onto the floor.

Taylor was spraying the area in front of our bunker with the machine gun, firing sudden bursts, then pausing, and then firing another burst.

I loaded another grenade in my launcher, pointed the barrel higher for more distance, and fired. This time, I stood upright at the window, hoping the grenade flash might show me the Viet Cong. But I saw no one as the grenade exploded. We stopped firing, and everything was quiet.

Davis and I stood peering out of the bunker window, not knowing what to expect next. After several tense minutes, a single bullet whistled through the window, hitting the rear wall. We both dove to the floor. Taylor, who was still outside, fired another burst from the machine gun.

He stopped shooting, and we listened again. There was no noise at all. We waited several minutes before speaking. "I think that last round was a good-night kiss from Charlie," Davis whispered. "At least, I hope it was."

We both laughed, but I could still see the fear in Davis' face, and I could still feel it in my gut. We waited impatiently, expecting more gunfire, but there was none. There was only the warm night air, the ghostly silence, and an unseen enemy somewhere out there in the darkness.

*Is it over? Are the Viet Cong retreating? Maybe they're pulling their dead or wounded through the rice paddies, retreating to the mountains?*

As the night dragged on, we realized the firefight was indeed over; it ended with that final bullet, one last attempt by Charlie to kill one of us. Had the Viet Cong heard one of us scream, it would have made their long retreat less tedious, but the Viet Cong had no way of knowing whether any of us lay dead or wounded. The thought brought a smile to my lips.

Soon Taylor joined us inside. We all seemed to breathe easier, despite the sweltering heat inside the bunker. We remained standing, staring out the window, looking for movement and listening.

Finally, the darkness began to fade, and the sun rose above the South China Sea, casting its soft, early-morning light on the rice paddies and nearby mountains. Landing Zone Bronco looked calm and peaceful once again, and the farmers would arrive soon with their water buffalo to begin work in the fields. We stepped outside and breathed the fresh air.

We began searching the area, looking for any debris from the spent claymores, leaving nothing for the Viet Cong to gather up and shape into a booby trap.

Then we looked for bodies, searching along the concertina wire and wading out into the rice paddies. But there were no dead Viet Cong anywhere. We also looked for bloodstains on the grass alongside the dikes, but there were none. It was like the Viet Cong had never been there.

The only sign of our firefight was a large bloodstain on Davis' T-shirt. It looked like he had been shot in the chest, but the blood was from a single splinter of wood shredded from the pole in the bunker when the Viet Cong first opened fire.

"Fucking splinter stabbed me in the chest," Davis said. He pulled up the bottom of his T-shirt so that he could see the cut. "Fucking wood chips were flying everywhere," he said. "I think I even swallowed one."

We all laughed as I stepped closer, pointing at the blood on Davis' T-shirt. "This is all we have to show for last night," I said, grinning. "That and my sore hand." I raised my hand, showing them the dark red bruise on my palm where I had slammed the flare tube.

"Holy shit, that's really swollen," Taylor said.

"Fucking dud flare," I said. "It was supposed to show us where the Viet Cong were hiding, and instead, it almost got us killed."

"Typical army equipment, a piece of shit," Davis said. He spit on the ground for emphasis.

We went back inside the bunker to get our gear. Before leaving, I examined the pole in the middle, its wood shredded near the top. Any one of us could have been struck by one of the bullets pouring through the window. We were incredibly lucky.

I closed the screen door at the back of the bunker, and the three of us began walking away. We walked in silence. We were exhausted, physically and emotionally, and we had no more words to say to one another.

8 January 1968
Duc Pho, Vietnam

Dear Mom and Dad,

I'm back at Duc Pho now, setting up the resupply for B Company. My supply line keeps getting stretched farther north as the company goes up in the mountains on search-and-destroy missions.

Tomorrow I'm going up to there to join the company. I'll be writing some combat loss reports for some of their equipment, including a starlight scope that was destroyed when a soldier tripped a booby trap. The booby trap ripped apart the starlight scope, but the soldier survived with no shrapnel. The medic, however, says he might lose his hearing from the blast.

A starlight scope is valued at $20,000, so I want to make sure I have all the proper paperwork. Plus, I hope there's some of the scope left so that I can take it back to base camp and give it to Warrant Officer Greenwood, the property officer.

I'm really anxious to get up north tomorrow and join the company. I haven't seen the company for a several days. Meanwhile, we've been receiving a lot of mortar here at night. The Viet Cong keep hitting the helicopter pads. But don't worry about me because my supply tent is a long way from the chopper pads. Plus, I'm becoming an expert at dogging mortar rounds (ha). Seriously, though, I'm safe as hell here in base camp.

Well, I have to get up at 5 a.m. to catch the chopper, so I'd better get some sleep. Keep the letters coming, and don't worry about me. I'll be fine.

> Your son,
> Alan

# Chapter 7

# The Tet Offensive

The Tet Offensive changed everything. I remember the exact moment it began. I was at the Marine Corps Air Base at Chu Lai with two other men from B Company to set up a forward supply station. It was night, and I was on my cot, looking up through the open flap at the top of the tent. Suddenly, there was a bright flash, a deafening explosion, and a blast of air pushing through the tent. The ground shook as more explosions rocked the area.

A Marine sergeant came rushing into the tent. "Get your gear and follow me," he shouted. "The Viet Cong are throwing rockets at the bomb dump."

We grabbed our weapons and ran outside. Another rocket slammed into the bomb dump, which was down the hill from our tent, near the runway. Bright flashes were lighting the night sky, and giant clouds of smoke began drifting across the runway.

We followed the sergeant to the bunker, went inside and found places to sit on the ground. The walls shook as more bombs exploded. Then we heard mortars landing nearby, and machine gun fire erupted at the perimeter.

*What the hell is going on?*

I had arrived in Chu Lai the day before on a convoy

from Landing Zone Bronco. As we passed through Duc Pho, we noticed the empty streets. The marketplace in the center of the village, normally a busy place in the morning, was almost deserted. When we drove out of Duc Pho onto Highway 1, there were only a few Vietnamese walking, or riding bicycles or motorbikes. The road was almost empty. Now, as I sat in the bunker listening to the exploding bombs and machine gun fire, I knew why there were so few people in Duc Pho and on the road. The Vietnamese knew something big was coming.

The exploding bombs seemed to be growing louder and more frequent. Each time there was another deafening blast, the ground shook, and we heard creaking noises coming from the roof of the bunker. Dust and sand began drifting down from the roof, and the air was suffocating. I stood to go outside, but a Marine standing guard at the doorway shook his head no. I sat back down on the ground.

Everyone in the bunker appeared restless as we sat waiting for the next ear-piercing blast. As the night wore on, the explosions slowly began to wane, but the heavy gunfire continued.

At sunrise, the gunfire stopped and a siren sounded the "all clear" signal. We stood and filed out of the bunker into drifting smoke, which soon began to clear. Looking down the hill at the air base runway, I saw another explosion at the bomb dump, with plumes of white smoke billowing up. The bomb dump was now a large, black, smoldering crater, still growing in size as more bombs burst from the heat. On the other side of the crater, the runway, stretched toward the ocean, its asphalt surface pockmarked by smaller craters. Two navy fighter jets sat at the far end of the runway, their wings torn off by mortar. On a landing pad next to the runway, a dozen helicopters were destroyed, their rotor blades twisted or torn from their mangled bodies. Smoke rose throughout the base from several demolished buildings and tents.

The hills bordering the base trapped the smoke on the ground, and it slowly drifted toward the ocean, dimming the morning sun into a grayish orange color. When the clouds of smoke passed, you could briefly see the blue ocean until another cloud approached, diming the sunshine.

As I stood looking at the devastation, a Marine stopped to watch another bomb explode. "They won't try to put that fire out," he said. "You can't go near it. Those bombs will be going up all day long."

The battered fighter jets and the mangled helicopters were an unsettling sight. There were almost no Marines visible anywhere, except for a few military police blocking the roads leading to the runway. Word soon came that the base was surrounded by Viet Cong and North Vietnamese forces in the nearby hills. As we returned to our tent, the mood was quiet, with little conversation. Everyone seemed to be wondering what would happen next. I had a single thought: *Could we end up like the French?*

I remembered a history class in college in which we studied the Indochina War. The French lost their war in Vietnam at the battle of Dien Bien Phu, when Vietnamese forces surrounded their base, bombarded it with artillery, and overran the perimeter.

Now, 14 years later, Chu Lai was surrounded by Viet

Cong and North Vietnamese troops on all sides, except where the base met the ocean. The similarities were unnerving.

*And now, what will happen to us?*

Adding to our fears, we learned from Armed Forces Radio that the North Vietnamese and Viet Cong had launched their surprise attacks all over South Vietnam, striking military bases and more than 100 cities and towns. The attacks, called the Tet Offensive, were highly coordinated, all beginning at the same time that night. The Viet Cong and North Vietnamese broke the ceasefire that was supposed to be in effect for the Vietnamese holiday of Tet (the Lunar New Year).

The fighting was fierce, but the American and South Vietnamese armies retained control over their base camps, and most of the cities. The Viet Cong and North Vietnamese controlled many of the rural areas.

In the days that followed, American and Vietnamese troops counter attacked throughout South Vietnam. In Chu Lai, Marines cautiously exited the base and began patrolling the surrounding countryside. There were daily skirmishes and firefights, but American and Vietnamese troops were slowly pushing the communists back toward their mountain hideouts. Mine-sweeping patrols soon began the dangerous task of clearing Highway 1, removing hundreds of booby traps and mines.

One month after I arrived in Chu Lai, I finally was given permission to return to my base camp at Duc Pho. I climbed aboard a truck, finding a place to sit on the wooden benches in the back. The truck was part of a convoy that passed through the base gate and onto

Highway 1. The trucks quickly accelerated to a fast speed, roaring down the road, horns blasting as we approached a village. The convoy sped through the village, leaving thick clouds of dust. There were no Vietnamese children rushing to the side of the road, begging for candy. Life still had not returned to normal.

Following the Tet Offensive, we felt more vulnerable, and the war looked increasingly hopeless. The Viet Cong and North Vietnamese had been chased back to the mountains, but so what? They'd be back.

Meanwhile, B Company was deployed to a new area south of Chu Lai in Quang Ngai province, which is why I had gone to Chu Lai to set up the forward supply line. US Army brass had decided it was time to try to pacify the hostile residents of the area. No one in B Company was happy about going to Quang Ngai, one of the most dangerous areas of South Vietnam. The South Vietnamese army had long since abandoned the district, leaving it to the control of village chiefs, the Viet Cong, and North Vietnamese army regulars. On military maps, the area had large areas colored pink, which designated it as a fortified or built-up area. We called it "Pinkville," but it was not a single village; it was a large area with several villages spread over several miles.

When I first arrived in Pinkville on the supply helicopter, several Vietnamese men were approaching B Company's firebase at the top of a hill. The Vietnamese carried bags of candy, offering the treats to Captain Lewis and his troops, asking that they, in turn, leave the area. It seemed like an audacious offer, but they were serious.

I could see the anger building in Captain Lewis' face

as he stared at the Vietnamese. "No way," he shouted. "We're here to win this goddamn war." The Vietnamese closed their bags of candy, turned, and left without saying another word. It seemed like an ominous sign of bad things to come.

Pinkville was mostly enemy territory. The pathways between villages were mined with booby traps, and when B Company troops approached the villages, they often came under fire. The Americans would return fire, make their way into the village, and interrogate the few residents they could find.

"Where are the VC?" the Americans asked. "Where did they go?"

"No VC here," the villagers would respond. "VC number 10." They would add "number 10," which meant the worst of all humans.

The men in B Company didn't believe the villagers, and as casualties mounted, frustration and anger grew. It soon reached the boiling point as more Americans fell dead or wounded, while villagers stood stone faced, proclaiming their innocence. Within six months of our arrival in Vietnam, the majority of the original members of B Company were gone, either killed or wounded, and their positions were filled with replacements.

The dead included Lieutenant Andy Moss, age 24, fresh out of officers' school. He led the Second Platoon through a rice paddy, avoiding a nearby path, which might have been mined. As they neared a village, a single shot rang out, hitting the lieutenant in the head and killing him instantly.

There was Sergeant Clyde Wilson, 31, a good old

"Southern boy" from Alabama, whom everyone liked. He was on patrol when he tripped a "bouncy betty" mine that sprung up and exploded, ripping the sergeant's body almost in half.

There was Private John Martell, 20, who was chasing a Viet Cong soldier through a thicket of trees when he stepped on a mine, which blew off both of his feet.

There was Corporal Marvin Jenner, 19, who was shot in the chest by a sniper. The medic rushed to his side and placed a compress on the wound, assuring the corporal that he would be okay. Jenner, however, went into shock and died somewhere above Pinkville as he was being evacuated by helicopter.

There was Private Martin Fernandez, age 20, a street-smart guy from Chicago. He was on perimeter guard when a mortar landed, blowing off both his legs, his right arm and blinding him in both eyes.

There was Private Ronald James, age 23, a recent graduate of the University of Michigan. James was a replacement. I issued him his M16 and gear and arranged for him to go to the field that afternoon on the supply helicopter. When he arrived in the field, James went to report to Captain Lewis, but the captain was talking on his radio and told James to go wait under a nearby tree. James went to the tree and sat down. A mine exploded, killing him. Later that day, someone estimated that James survived for less than 10 minutes in the field.

Most of the B Company's casualties shared common characteristics. They were young, they often were draftees, and most did not want to be sent to Vietnam.

Each time someone died, Harris would make his way

to the morgue to identify the body, and I would gather the dead man's personal belongings, place them in an envelope, and mail the envelope to his family. The tedium of the brutal war continued.

It was bound to happen sooner or later. One day, several replacements arrived at my supply tent just as I was preparing to inventory the personal belongings of four soldiers who had been killed. The personal items were in boxes on the floor. I was getting ready to go through the things with a clerk named Corporal Paul Chandler, when the replacements suddenly walked into the tent. The new troops stared at us and at the items in the boxes, but they said nothing.

"Don't end up like these guys," Chandler warned them, a sadistic smirk on his face.

I saw the confused, anxious looks on the replacements' faces, and as I turned toward Chandler, my anger was growing.

"Shut the fuck up," I whispered to him.

Two weeks later, on a steamy night in April, I was on guard duty in a bunker near the POW compound. As usual, I had picked Taylor and Davis to be on guard duty with me. We followed the same routine, first searching the bunker for booby traps and poisonous critters in the sandbags. Then we set up our machine gun outside on the side of the bunker and placed the claymore mines out front.

On this night, we learned the bunker next to us would be manned by ARVN troops. We all frowned when we saw the Vietnamese soldiers arrive before sundown.

"Oh, for Christ's sake, ARVNs for neighbors," Davis

said, groaning.

The ARVNs had a bad reputation among American troops, but not because they were tough guys. It was the opposite: they were incompetent, poorly trained, lacked discipline, and frequently deserted. They were awful soldiers.

As darkness approached, the ARVNs seemed oblivious to the danger around them. They were drinking rice wine in the bunker, smoking in the open where the Viet Cong could see their lit cigarettes, and talking in loud voices. Then I saw several village girls make their way through the concertina wire and into the bunker. Soon a portable radio was playing Vietnamese music. The ARVNs were doing everything they could to make themselves a target.

"Shit, this is really bad," I said. "Those ARVNs are going to get their asses blown away."

"I don't give a fuck about the ARVNs," Davis said. "I'm worried they will attract sappers to the perimeter, and we're right next door."

We all nodded yes. I considered calling base command center to tell them our concerns, but I didn't have a good rapport with the center, especially after the night I called Sergeant Trujillo a shithead. As often was the case in Vietnam, we would try to solve this problem on our own.

"Okay, I'll go talk to them," I said.

"Di di mau [go quickly]," Taylor said. "Before the sappers get here."

Davis and Taylor were both laughing as I stepped out of our bunker and began walking to the ARVNs' bunker.

When I arrived, I stopped outside the door at the rear of the bunker.

"Hello," I said in a loud voice. "Anyone home?"

Several ARVNs came out of the bunker and smiled at me. They all wore loose-fitting khakis uniforms and appeared to be very young.

I pointed to the growing darkness in front of their bunker and said, "VC might come." Then I dragged my finger across my throat.

The ARVNs nodded, and some laughed.

"Please be careful and look for Viet Cong," I said, waving my arm in a broad motion toward the rice paddies.

The ARVNs smiled and laughed again, and then they were quiet. I didn't know what else to say, and after an awkward silence, I waved good-bye and left.

Arriving back at my bunker, Taylor and Davis turned to look at me.

"So how'd that go?" Taylor asked.

"Not worth a damn," I said.

"You mean they're not going to keep a close watch for Charlie tonight?" asked Davis in a sarcastic voice.

"That's the last of their concerns," I said. "Their first concern is to get laid by the girls in their bunker, and their second concern is probably smoking some good dope. So we're going to keep a close watch tonight, including the area in front of *their* bunker."

Davis made a loud groaning noise. "Fucking ARVNs," he said.

Soon we settled into our bunker guard routine, Davis agreeing to take the first watch; Taylor, the second watch;

and me, the third.

There was cloud cover, and the night was very dark. Inside the bunker, it was hot as usual. Sleep was impossible, and we all stood at the bunker window, talking in hushed voices.

"How was R&R in Bangkok?" I asked Taylor.

"Number one," he said. "I met this girl named Lamai in the hotel bar, and we banged all week long. I thought my pecker was going to fall off."

We all laughed as quietly as possible, and then Taylor continued.

"She even took me to her parents' home outside Bangkok," he said. "Mama son made a nice big dinner, and we drank lots of rice wine. It was great."

Taylor paused and spit out the bunker window. "And you know, there are no commie troops in Thailand. Lamai said that if any communists showed up in her village, the locals would report them right away to the police."

Our conversation stopped. The heat was suffocating inside the bunker, draining our energy. It felt like there was no air to breathe.

The hot night wore on, and hours later, the ARVNs' party apparently ended. The loud laughter faded away, and the only sound was the Vietnamese music still playing on their portable radio.

"Maybe they decided it was time to start watching for Charlie," Davis said.

"They're not looking for anything," Taylor said. "Fucking ARVNs are probably sleeping."

The hours passed, and everything was quiet on the perimeter. When it was my turn to stand guard, I stood alone at the bunker window. I felt exhausted from the heat, but I also felt tense, scanning the area in front of the ARVNs' bunker.

*The dumb shits are probably passed out.*

As I stared into the darkness, I could see almost nothing, and there was no noise, not even the occasional frog croaking in the rice paddies. A bead of perspiration slid down my forehead, dropping onto my hand and causing me to flinch. I was nervous knowing the ARVNs were likely sleeping, which meant I was the only one awake and guarding that sector of the perimeter. I had the sudden urge to awaken Davis and Taylor. But when I looked down, they were both sleeping. Taylor was snoring. I would let them sleep, at least for now.

Time passed slowly, until finally the darkness began to fade. I knew sunrise was not far off, and the tension began to ease inside me. Everything was quiet on the perimeter. Soon the farmers would arrive with their water buffalo to begin work in the fields.

Unknown to me, there was something else on the perimeter. Hidden in the fading darkness was a group of Viet Cong sappers who had spent hours patiently crawling through the rice fields, carefully holding their explosives above the surface of the water.

The sappers' movement was slow, silent, and deliberate, but they'd finally reached their target. They lay in front of the ARVN bunker, preparing their bags of explosives, waiting for the right moment.

There were two loud explosions. The ground shook, and debris flew up from the bunker.

"What the fuck!" Taylor shouted. He and Davis

jumped up and stood next to me at the window.

We couldn't see any movement in the ARVN bunker—we saw only thick clouds of smoke spilling out. Moments later, the debris from the explosion began falling down on our bunker roof and splashing into the rice paddy. Once the debris stopped falling, there was complete silence.

"Son of a bitch, we've got sappers out there!" I screamed. "I'm blowing the claymore on the right!"

We all ducked as I detonated the claymore. The ground shook, and we stood and opened fire with our M16s, spraying the area in front of the ARVN bunker and then swinging to the left to spray the area in front of our bunker. We fired frantically into the fading darkness.

"Take that, you fuckers," Taylor screamed. When he turned toward me, I motioned for him to stop firing. I cupped my ear, signaling that we should listen for any movement. We all stood wide-eyed, staring out the bunker window, but there was no sound at all.

"Fucking sappers are still here!" I could hear the panic in my voice. "I'm blowing claymore two. Take cover!"

We all ducked as the second explosion rocked our bunker. Then we opened fire again with our M16s.

The bunker landline phone rang, and I answered it.

"This is Sergeant Trujillo. Hold your fire!" His voice sounded icy and commanding. "I've got a squad coming out of the POW compound to see what's happening in the ARVN bunker."

"Yes sir," I said.

We stopped shooting. A door opened on the compound wall, and several soldiers rushed out. Two took up positions in front of the ARVN bunker, lying on the ground, their weapons facing the rice paddies. The others went inside the bunker and searched for survivors. Word came later that all five ARVNs were dead, along with three girls from the village.

We could hear the American soldiers cursing as they rummaged through the bunker, searching for clues about the sappers' explosives.

The sun was rising, but we waited several minutes before stepping out of our bunker. Then we began canvassing the area in front, picking up debris and searching for dead sappers, but there were none. I looked to the nearby mountains, wondering where the sappers were at that moment. I was sure they were having a happy retreat, discussing their successful attack and talking in excited, animated voices. Planning future attacks.

I closed the back door to our bunker, and the three of us walked to the ARVN bunker. Its roof was gone, blown off by the explosions, and we stared at the bloody mess of tangled bodies. The stench of blood and torn bodies was overpowering.

Several medics arrived with stretchers and began carrying the dead to a nearby truck. We turned and walked away, moving quickly, anxious to get away from the smell.

"What a fucking mess," Taylor said, shaking his head.

"They brought it on themselves," Davis said.

"I tried to talk to them," I said. "But they wouldn't listen."

Our conversation was hard and calloused, with no

room for emotions. As we walked, I glanced at Taylor and Davis. They both looked tired, worn out, and much older than they really were. Taylor was 19 years old—a kid really—only one year out of high school. Davis was age 20 and hoping to attend college when he got out of the army. I was 23, one year out of college, and the "old man" of our group.

"Jesus, that smell was bad," Davis said, shaking his head.

"I wouldn't want to pull guard duty there tonight," Taylor said. "No fucking way."

As we walked, I also thought of the dead Vietnamese. They were young like us, and they probably had dreams for the future. Now they were dead, but when we looked at their bodies, we didn't see them entirely as victims. We blamed them for their own deaths. I wondered how we had become so hardened. Maybe our cynical attitudes were there to guard our sanity, a desperate, perverted attempt to somehow feel normal in a place where the killing never stopped.

In the weeks that followed, a feeling of hopelessness seemed to spread everywhere, a dark, suffocating mood. I often heard soldiers complain, "What the fuck are we doing here?"

There was almost no joking or horseplay among troops. The sound of laughter was gone. And when a soldier did laugh out loud, it seemed like a strange, unfitting sound. Adding to the despair, nothing changed in Vietnam. The hot, tedious days were often followed by harrowing nights. As the number of casualties continued to grow, more replacements arrived at my supply tent.

On the nights when I didn't have bunker duty, I often sat alone in my tent, sometimes smoking marijuana from the orphanage, wondering what was happening back in the world, our expression for home.

I pictured families sitting down to dinner in a lighted room or perhaps driving to the theater to see a movie, with no mines buried in the road or snipers hiding in the bushes. Maybe life in America was as constant and unchanging as it was in Vietnam?

According to the news reports on Armed Services Radio, the American government was unwavering in its determination to continue the war.

The reports said most members in Congress still believed we could win the battle, stopping the communist advance in Southeast Asia. But those of us in Vietnam knew this wasn't true. We would never win this war, and we wondered how our government could be so ignorant.

The war would be determined by the topography of Vietnam. The mountains towered over the coastal plains, some peaks rising more than 8,000 feet near the borders of Laos and Cambodia. The highlands were covered with thick jungle, providing a perfect camouflaged refuge for the Viet Cong and North Vietnamese troops. From their mountain hideouts, they could easily sweep down onto the coastal areas to attack the South Vietnamese and American troops.

The fate of the war was also etched in the faces of many Vietnamese. In Duc Pho, I often saw the hard, glaring looks of the villagers as they stared at us with a silent death wish—or at best, a wish that we would leave their country. I wondered what a group of American congressmen might think if they saw those expressions. Or what would a congressman think if he accompanied B Company on a patrol through Pinkville?

But, of course, none of that would ever happen. Instead, the American politicians would sit in their air-conditioned offices in Washington, reading intelligence reports and shaking their heads over the rising casualties.

But in the end, they would continue to send thousands more young men to Vietnam, only to be slaughtered, along with even greater numbers of Vietnamese.

Adding to my own despair, a dark realization was growing inside me. I was forced to acknowledge that I played a role in the war that I hated so much.

As the company supply sergeant, I would continue to equip the young men arriving at my tent, assigning them weapons and gear, preparing them for battle, and transporting them to the field. I was a small but important link in the whole deadly process.

I couldn't ignore my supply role anymore, but I tried not to think about it. And during those moments when I did think about it, I had a ready excuse: *Fuck it. If I don't do it, someone else will. The army will make sure of that.*

Still, there were times when I sat alone in my tent at night, and the hard reality of Vietnam overwhelmed me. They were my darkest moments, with thoughts so disturbing that I shared them with no one.

I felt guilty because I knew that some of the replacements I equipped and sent to the field might die.

I felt guilty because I knew I might live.

11 March 1968
Duc Pho, Vietnam

Dear Carol and Wally,

I've got war on my mind over here because Charlie keeps reminding me every night. He stepped up his mortar and rocket attacks and destroyed all the supply tents in the 2nd Battalion last week. They've also been throwing a lot of satchel charges in bunkers on the perimeter.

Three nights ago, I was on bunker guard, and Charlie hit again with another mortar attack. The next morning, I went to see a friend in the helicopter company and found him wounded. A mortar landed only 10 feet from him, but he only got shrapnel in one leg. A medic and I carried him on a stretcher to the helicopter.

There was another mortar attack last night, and one of the guys who was killed was due to leave here today and go back to the United States. What a shame.

I'm getting shorter every day, but not fast enough. I have 160 days to go, but I'll never be able to relax until I get out of here, and my jet touches down back in the world.

Our company has had bad luck the last two weeks.

*Several men stepped on mines and booby traps. One guy stepped on an undetonated 500-pound bomb that the Viet Cong had found and buried in the ground; they couldn't find any remains. Replacements are being assigned to B Company, but we're still short of troops.*

*Well, I've talked enough about the war. Keep the letters coming. In the meantime, I'll keep dodging those mortar rounds.*

*Alan*

13 March 1968
Duc Pho, Vietnam

Dear Mom and Dad,

I realize the correspondence has been slow from this end, but it's the same story here — I'm staying very busy supplying the company. I appreciate you writing as often as you do, and I'll try to keep up better on this end.

As far as the war goes, it's the same old drag. The hot, dry season is here, and Charlie has been mortaring us less frequently, but he still manages to throw in a few rounds now and then.

A friend was wounded by a mortar round the other night. He has some shrapnel in his leg, but he'll be okay. Several in our company have also been wounded in recent weeks, but many of them will be okay.

Meanwhile, I might be able to go to rest and recuperation (R&R) in Australia in May. I know the clerk who handles the paperwork, so he should be able to fix it up for me. Normally, when you're as short as I am, you can't get R&R. I applied for Sydney as my first choice, my second choice is Bangkok, and the third is Tokyo. All of them beat the hell out of being here in Duc Pho.

Keep the letters coming. Your son,

Alan

# Chapter 8

# Pray for Peace

The casualty rate in B Company soared as the company continued its patrols through Pinkville. As required by the army, Harris kept meticulous records on the casualties and almost everything else that happened in B Company. Harris was also the man to see if you wanted to apply for R&R, receive medical treatment, or see the brigade dentist. But perhaps his hardest job was graves registration officer, which Harris shared with me.

Harris would glumly walk into my tent and announce, "We've got more KIAs," the acronym for killed in action. Harris would go to the morgue and identify the dead, and I would gather and inventory their personal effects to send to their families. It was a depressing, methodical process with no end in sight.

As B Company's casualties continued to grow, more replacements were arriving at my tent. I often looked out the doorway and watched them approach. I felt hollow inside, lacking emotion as I handed them their gear and asked them to sign for their weapons. Most of the time, I tried to avoid much conversation, but sometimes I had no choice.

"Hey, Sarge, how goes the war around here?" The

new soldier spoke with a calm voice as I handed him his gear.

"It's not going very well," I said. "We've had lots of casualties, mostly guys stepping on booby traps and mines. It's like walking on broken glass out there, so be real careful."

The soldier's face turned somber, and he nodded. He stood in front of me as though he expected me to say more, but I only stared at him. He was tall and slim, his hair a crew cut. He was probably not long out of high school, another boy being sent to war.

"Graduated recently?" I asked.

"Last May," he answered. "How about you?"

His question surprised me, and I had to stop and think. "Umm, yeah, I graduated in August over a year ago."

"You graduated from high school in August?" he asked.

"No, it was college," I answered. "University of North Dakota."

"North Dakota. You're the first guy I've met from there."

"I hear that a lot," I said. "There aren't many of us."

He laughed, signed for his M16, gathered his gear, and left the supply tent. I watched him walk down the path to a nearby tent where he would spend the night. He had a confident stride, his shoulders held high. But to me, he looked young, innocent, and vulnerable. I silently wished him well, and I hoped I would never see this young man again.

One month later, the young man returned, this time in a body bag. Harris identified his remains, and I inventoried his personal items. It was obvious that there would be no end to this gruesome process. Nor would the replacements stop coming. Harris handled all of the replacements' paperwork, and I gave them their gear. Everything would continue as usual.

Harris and I never once talked to each other about this depressing procedure, this useless attempt to put back what was taken from B Company. We knew there was no point in complaining to each other or to anyone else. It wouldn't change anything.

So we mourned the dead, cursed the politicians in Washington, and longed for the day when we could leave Vietnam. And if we survived the war, we would take our secret thoughts home and seldom share them with anyone.

Meanwhile, as the casualties continued to grow in Pinkville, the military brass decided it was time to do something different to make the villagers less hostile. The brigade assigned a "pacification officer," a captain named John Stover. He was a tall, thin man with a trimmed mustache and a scholarly look. He looked out of place next to the infantry officers, but he didn't seem to care.

The captain was stationed at a hillside encampment called Fire Base Dottie, about three miles inland from the

Pinkville area. As soon as Captain Stover arrived, he began making frequent visits to the nearby villages, asking the Vietnamese if they'd seen the Viet Cong and offering them cash payments for bringing him mines or booby traps.

Within days, Captain Stover was collecting all sorts of armaments every time he drove into a village. It appeared that his plan was working and that Captain Stover might even make Pinkville a less dangerous place.

He also tried to soften the American troops' hardened attitudes toward the villagers. He began accompanying infantrymen on their patrols, talking about the US Army's mission and explaining the dilemma facing the villagers, whom he said were caught between two opposing forces: the communists and the noncommunists.

"What would you do if you were in their shoes?" the captain asked.

"But those fucking gooks in the villages are always trying to kill us," a soldier from B Company complained. "They set mines and booby traps on the trails and shoot at us when we approach their villages."

Captain Stover angrily shook his head at the soldier. "You're wrong; it's the Viet Cong that's firing at you, not the villagers. And by the way, they're not gooks, they're Vietnamese people!"

As the weeks went by, Captain Stover decided it was time to step up his pacification campaign. Each morning, often before sunrise, the captain drove his jeep out of camp, following the rough, dusty trails leading to the villages. It was an incredibly dangerous thing to do, especially by himself. The infantrymen in the perimeter bunkers shook their heads as they watched the captain drive off into the darkness.

The captain's actions soon earned him an assorted reputation. Some said he was courageous, but others saw him as a misguided idealist. Some thought the captain was a combination of the two.

Still, no matter what others thought of him, the captain had an enduring quality, which won him grudging respect from most. Although soldiers might disagree with the captain over who was shooting at whom, everyone agreed that the captain was responsible for the removal of many mines and booby traps. That was a good thing.

Meanwhile, the captain's cache of mines and booby traps was growing. Word spread throughout Pinkville of the cash-for-armaments program, and when Captain Stover drove into a village, there was always a small crowd waiting for him.

On a steamy day in May, the captain drove to a small village near the South China Sea. The captain got out of his jeep and began his usual routine, paying villagers as they brought mines and booby traps to him. As the captain placed the armaments in the back of his jeep, an American infantry patrol entered the village and watched the captain go into a nearby hooch to talk to the village chief, asking if he had seen any Viet Cong in the area in recent days.

"No VC," the chief assured the captain. "VC number ten," the chief said, spitting on the ground for emphasis.

The captain smiled, handed the village chief some money, and stepped out of the hooch, shielding his eyes from the blazing sun. The booby traps and mines remained securely stacked in the back of his jeep. The villagers were gone, probably because of the heat.

The captain waved good-bye to the American infantrymen on the far side of the village and walked to his jeep, sliding into the driver's seat and starting the engine.

The explosion rocked the village, sending a giant cloud of white smoke mushrooming above the huts. The pacification officer was gone in an instant, and when the infantrymen later searched the area, they found no remains of Captain Stover anywhere.

Later that day, when word came from Fire Base Dottie of the pacification officer's death, there were few words of sympathy in B Company. Instead there were mostly cynical comments, especially from the soldier who had been lectured by the captain only days before.

"Those gooks done blew the captain away," he said, laughing.

The brigade decided not to replace Captain Stover, but replacements would continue to arrive for infantrymen who were killed or wounded. However, the replacements didn't arrive fast enough, and as summer approached, there were only about 80 infantrymen in B Company, a big drop from the 120 infantrymen when they arrived in Vietnam. Pinkville, with its booby traps, mines, and snipers, was extracting a heavy toll on our company.

The man who was most distressed by the loss of American lives was Colonel Binder, although perhaps not for the normal reasons. Colonel Binder still dreamed of being promoted to general, and he worried that it might not look good when so many of his men were falling in battle. Furthermore, as more of his troops were killed or wounded, the number of enemy killed began to drop. That was not good at all.

"I need more kills!" the colonel shouted at his weekly staff meeting inside his tent at Fire Base Dottie. He would quiz his company commanders as to what was going on in the field.

"We're short of men," Captain Lewis complained. "And the replacements aren't arriving fast enough."

Colonel Binder glared at the captain but said nothing.

The next morning, the colonel boarded his helicopter and flew out over the countryside, searching for the enemy. If his troops couldn't kill Charlie, then he would. In the weeks that followed, the colonel also began flying overhead as his troops patrolled the ground below. The colonel would make frequent calls to officers on the ground, asking them how things were going down there.

Members of C Company were on patrol one day when the colonel's helicopter appeared overhead. The colonel was on the radio, talking to Captain Jason Becker below, when the helicopter suddenly drew small-arms fire.

"Charlie One, where's the fire coming from?" the colonel asked. "Maybe we can help from up here."

"Nothing's happening down here," Captain Becker responded. "All quiet in the bush."

Several more rounds were fired at the helicopter, with one bullet lodging in the side door.

The helicopter pilots turned, facing the colonel and motioning that it was time to leave. The colonel nodded yes, and the helicopter circled above the rice paddies and began flying back to camp.

On the ground below, two soldiers from C Company watched in dismay as the colonel's helicopter flew away. They were the ones who were shooting at the helicopter.

Word soon spread among infantrymen of the attempt on the colonel's life. Soldiers agreed that it might be easy to secretly shoot at the colonel's helicopter. Infantry companies were often spread out over a wide distance in Pinkville. A soldier in an outward flank might fire several shots, and no one would know.

In the weeks that followed, Colonel Binder's helicopter was reportedly shot at several more times. Luckily for the colonel and the others on board, the helicopter always returned safely to base camp. Unbeknown to Colonel Binder, he had become a target. Some of his own men were trying to kill him.

After five months in Vietnam, Caption Lewis applied for R&R in Hawaii, where he would meet his wife. Two weeks before his departure, he summoned Lieutenant Andrew O'Connor to the field. O'Connor was the company's executive officers and would lead B Company in the captain's absence.

Lieutenant O'Connor was a quiet, serious man who seldom smiled. He started his army career as a "lifer" and planned a full military career up to retirement, but now he was having second thoughts. The Vietnam War was starting to wear heavily on Lieutenant O'Connor, especially with the soaring casualties suffered by B Company in Pinkville.

Lieutenant O'Connor decided the war was a futile campaign, a waste of life. He was also disgusted by the attitudes of some officers, including Colonel Binder, who he thought were more concerned with their military careers than the welfare of their troops.

In contrast, Captain Lewis, the career officer, believed in the war. He believed the Americans and South Vietnamese would eventually defeat the communists. Captain Lewis also cared about the welfare of his troops, but he believed there were sacrifices to be made in war. If Captain Lewis had been ordered to move his company into a dangerous area of Pinkville, he would have gone without questioning the order.

Meanwhile, Colonel Binder continued to pore over his maps of Pinkville. He often ordered B Company to patrol the most dangerous areas, hoping it would result in a higher number of enemy killed.

B Company was setting up a defensive perimeter one morning on a hillside near Pinkville when the colonel's helicopter approached and landed. The colonel jumped out and quickly strode to where the Captain Lewis and Lieutenant O'Connor stood. The three exchanged salutes and then the colonel pulled out his map, pointing to a certain area.

"We need your company to sweep through Hien Luong," the colonel said. "Intelligence says there might be a battalion of Viet Cong in that area. So we want to hit them first, before they come after us."

Captain Lewis nodded his head in agreement, but Lieutenant O'Connor was unmoving.

"Sir, that's the area where A Company got torn to shit two weeks ago," the lieutenant said. "It seems to me that we need more than one infantry company to take them on. Especially now that we're short of men."

The colonel looked up from his map and stared hard at the lieutenant. His lips tightened, and his face looked angry.

"If we wait until everything is perfect on our side, the Viet Cong will be gone by the time we decide to attack," the colonel said. There was a hard mocking tone to his voice.

"I'm less worried about the Viet Cong getting away than I am about the potential casualties in our company," Lieutenant O'Connor said.

"War is hell, lieutenant," the colonel said. "I'm sure you've heard that before, but it's still true."

"When do you want us to begin our sweep of the area?" asked Captain Lewis, anxious to end the dispute between the colonel and his executive officer.

"Begin tomorrow," the colonel said. He folded up his map. The three exchanged salutes, and the colonel strode to his helicopter.

Early the next morning, B Company began heading toward Hien Luong. The company moved down a hillside and into the rice paddies, avoiding the pathways and narrow trails.

By late afternoon, the company neared the northern edge of Hien Luong, which sat in the middle of a wide plain of rice fields. So far, the day had been uneventful. There was only the hot blazing sun and the sloshing sounds of the soldiers' boots as they moved through the rice paddies.

Suddenly, there was a burst of gunfire from the village. Two soldiers fell wounded and screaming into the water.

"Get into the hedgerows!" Captain Lewis shouted.

Gunfire erupted from several hooches, and several more Americans fell. The infantrymen scattered in all directions, moving to the nearest hedgerow or seeking shelter behind rice-paddy dikes, dragging the wounded men with them through the water.

Medic John Silva crawled to the side of Sergeant Andrew Fonte, the most seriously wounded, and placed a compress on the bullet wound near his shoulder.

"You got it in the shoulder, Sarge, but you're going to be all right." Silva shouted the words, hoping the sergeant could hear him above the gunfire.

Sergeant Fonte said nothing. His eyes were becoming glazed, and his body was limp. The sergeant was going into shock, and the medic knew that shock could kill him.

The medic placed his hands on both sides of the sergeant's head and shook him to get his attention. "I said you're going to be all right!" he shouted. Sergeant Fonte's body jerked, and his eyes seemed to focus on the medic's face.

"My boys are back home," the sergeant said. "I can't leave my boys. What will they do without me?" Tears began flowing down the sergeant's face, and then they stopped. The anguished look faded from the sergeant's face and his eyes began to glaze over again.

"Stay awake!" the medic shouted. "You're going to be all right!"

There was no response from the sergeant. His body became limp, and he stopped breathing. Silva tried to revive him, but it was hopeless. Silva left the sergeant and crawled to another wounded man and put a compress on his leg. The medic shouted some words as he worked, but his words were lost in the heavy gunfire.

The gunfire continued from the village for several

minutes, and then it stopped. The Americans waited in the hedgerows and behind the dikes. There was no sound except for a rooster crowing somewhere nearby. Captain Lewis radioed for a helicopter evacuation of the wounded men and ordered a squad to move into the village. The men moved slowly and carefully, scanning the area as they moved. Soon they disappeared into the thatched huts. Ten minutes later, several troops appeared at the edge of the village. "It's deserted," they said. "There's no one here."

The company began moving into the clustered huts, keeping a watchful eye for booby traps and snipers. They found four dead Viet Cong, their bodies riddled with bullets. B Company completed its sweep through the village, finding no one else. The company's toll from the firefight was one dead, (Sergeant Fonte) and seven wounded. While waiting for the helicopters to arrive, the captain made his rounds, talking to the wounded. He also stopped and stood over Sergeant Fonte's body; it appeared he was offering a prayer. For a brief moment, it looked like Captain Lewis was about to cry, but then his face straightened, and his demeanor changed.

"I want this whole goddamn village torched," he told Lieutenant O'Connor. "I don't want one goddamn thing left standing."

"Yes sir," said the lieutenant. He organized a squad, and they spread out, using their cigarette lighters to set the hooches on fire.

Soon the village was a growing fireball, the flames

jumping from one thatched hut to the next. The lieutenant stood watching the inferno with the others, a grim look on his face. The lieutenant blamed everything on Colonel Binder—the dead, the wounded, and now the burning village. None of this would have happened, he thought, had the colonel not pointed to an area on his map and ordered B Company to move into the area.

Once the casualties were radioed to Colonel Binder, he probably expected the military brass to question him about the operation, especially since B Company was plagued by more casualties than other units. The colonel had already decided that ordering B Company to sweep through Hien Luong was worth the risk. Unfortunately, only four enemy were found dead, but Colonel Binder could easily inflate that number, assuming the Viet Cong dragged at least a half dozen of their dead into the jungle. Colonel Binder would also argue that Hien Luong was no longer a threat, making all of Pinkville a safer place.

One week later, Captain Lewis prepared to leave B Company for R&R in Hawaii, where he would meet his wife. I arranged transportation for the captain on a reconnaissance spotter plane that was flying from Duc Pho to Da Nang, where he would board the jetliner.

The captain and I climbed into the supply jeep and headed for the airstrip. As I drove, I noticed that the captain's mood was unusually quiet. When we arrived at the runway, the captain got out of the jeep, holding his duffle bag, and turned as if to say thanks, but no words came out of his mouth. The captain stared at me in silence.

He looked spent. His officer demeanor was gone, as he stood alone on the runway. The war was obviously wearing heavily on Captain Lewis, and he would carry this burden with him to his R&R in Hawaii. We continued staring at each other, saying nothing for several awkward moments. I thought I saw the captain's lips move slightly, but still no words came out of his mouth. I felt I should break the silence.

"Enjoy Hawaii, sir!" I shouted at the captain. "And don't worry about any of the shit around here; it will still be here when you get back." The captain waved good-bye, a thin, tenuous smile on his face.

The following day, Colonel Binder's helicopter landed at Landing Zone Bronco for repairs. The colonel contacted Lieutenant O'Connor and said he wanted to meet him in the B Company clerk's tent. Harris asked me to join him at the meeting, mostly because Harris didn't want to be the only enlisted man at the meeting.

At exactly 1400, the colonel walked into the tent, and we saluted him. The colonel pulled his map out of his pocket and got right down to business.

"We've got intelligence reports of one, maybe two Viet Cong infantry companies gathering in the Hoa Phu area," the colonel said to Lieutenant O'Connor. "And there might be a third company of North Vietnamese Regulars there for support.

"First thing tomorrow morning, I want you to lead B Company to Hoa Phu and engage the enemy." The colonel's face was hard and determined. "Beat the hell out of them. Get rid of them for good!"

The two officers were facing each other, while Harris and I looked mostly at the floor. Then came the bombshell.

"No sir," Lieutenant O'Connor said.

An icy silence settled over the tent as Harris and I exchanged nervous glances. The lieutenant and colonel were staring at each other, their faces hardened.

"I'm not taking B Company to that area of Pinkville," the lieutenant added.

"What?" the colonel shouted.

"I'm not taking B Company into that deathtrap," the lieutenant said. "They'd be chopped to pieces!"

"Lieutenant O'Connor, I'm giving you an order!" The colonel shouted his words, his facing turning bright red.

"I don't care what you're ordering," the lieutenant said. "I'm not taking the company to Hoa Phu."

"You're refusing an order?"

"That's right, sir," said Lieutenant O'Connor. "And you're not going to do a goddamn thing about it."

The colonel looked stunned, like the air had suddenly been sucked out of his lungs. His lips were drawn tight, his eyes piercing and cold. He looked like he wanted to kill Lieutenant O'Connor. The colonel turned and walked out of the tent.

The lieutenant looked at Harris and me. "Colonel

Binder isn't going to do anything. I've got more shit on him than the shit piled in one of those latrines outside. He's stretched the limits, sending B Company into areas where there are large numbers of Viet Cong. I could hang him by the balls, and he knows it."

Lieutenant O'Connor walked out of the tent. Harris went to the door and glanced out to make sure the lieutenant was gone. "Son of a bitch, can you believe it?"

"No, I can't! What the hell?"

Harris shrugged his shoulders. "All I know is that everyone is sick and tired of this fucking war."

I left Harris and began walking back to my supply tent. I felt energized after witnessing the tense exchange between officers. Lieutenant O'Connor had refused the colonel's orders. He said what other officers probably wanted to say, but they didn't have the courage.

In the week that followed, Lieutenant O'Connor led B Company on pacification patrols through villages near the edge of Pinkville. The area was not heavily fortified, and there were no casualties. Also missing was the colonel's helicopter flying overhead.

Days later, Captain Lewis returned from R&R. As he jumped off the helicopter at Landing Zone Bronco, Colonel Binder was waiting for him. The colonel got right down to business, pulling his map out of his pocket and showing the captain where his next mission would be.

It might be a dangerous maneuver, the colonel warned, but this was Vietnam, for Christ's sake, and there would be sacrifices if they were going to win this war.

Captain Lewis nodded his head yes.

20 April 1968
Duc Pho, Vietnam

Dear Mom and Dad,

Last week we received 41 replacements for our company, so I worked long hours getting them equipped and arranging transportation to the field.

I hope they reach some kind of peace agreement soon in Paris to end this war. I don't want to see more Americans sent to this godforsaken place. I don't think the Vietnam War is worth one more American life, but then I'm biased, since I'm here, seeing it all.

Meanwhile, we heard on Armed Services Radio about the assassination of Martin Luther King, the riots that followed, and federal troops being called in to protect the capitol building and White House. It sounds like our country is falling apart, but we're still over here saving the world from the communists. It all seems so senseless.

There has been little action here lately. Charlie seems to have run out of mortar shells, and they haven't been harassing our perimeter so much at night. Hopefully it will stay that way. However, our company was hit pretty hard last month up north.

We lost a platoon leader, a platoon sergeant, and a couple of others. Since our company has arrived in Vietnam, we've had a 40 percent turnover, but many of the wounded will be okay, especially when they get evacuated from this hellhole.

It's harvest time in Vietnam, but it's not a harvest like you would have at home. As the farmers harvest their rice from the paddies, the ARVNs have been hanging around to keep the Viet Cong and North Vietnamese regulars from stealing it.

I'm looking forward to my upcoming R&R in Australia. By the time I return from R&R I'll have only 90 days to go to ETS. So I'll begin training a new supply sergeant to take over. For the first time in the army, I'm beginning to feel real short. Lieutenant O'Connor did a great job of leading B Company last week (there were no casualties at all). The lieutenant took over while Captain Lewis was on R&R in Hawaii. As soon as the captain came back, however, our company was ordered to begin patrols on the peninsula south of Chu Lai. It's a bad area, and we've had many casualties there.

It seems like nothing changes in Vietnam. I wish I could think of other things to write about, but ever since I arrived here, my life has been the same. The army and the war — that's all I know.

Pray for peace,

Alan

Sergeant Alan Quale sits with B Company supplies
after arriving in Duc Pho, Vietnam.

B Company troops relax on the deck of US Navy ship
en route from Hawaii to South Vietnam.

Highway 1, above, stretches through the marketplace in Duc Pho, which was considered to be a "friendly" village.

The view from the helicopter above the rice fields in South Vietnam.

Looking out the window of a bunker at Landing Zone Bronco. The lines in the photo are chicken wire strung to deflect grenades and other explosives. The bunker exterior is shown below.

# Chapter 9

# R&R in Sydney

There are some images from Vietnam that I will never forget, including standing in a long line of troops at the military airport in Da Nang, waiting to board a jetliner bound for R&R in Sydney, Australia. As we shuffled forward, I saw a doctor sitting behind a small wooden table at the foot of the steps leading up to the aircraft.

When I neared the front of the line, a medic approached.

"Drop your drawers so that the doctor can examine your penis," the medic commanded. "You can't go to Australia without this examination."

As I approached the front of the line, I obediently dropped my pants.

"Name?" the doctor asked.

"Alan Quale."

The doctor searched the manifest, found my name, and then wrote my name on a small slip of paper.

"Move up to the table," he said.

When I approached, he reached up and grabbed my penis and examined it. Then he wrote something on the slip of paper and handed it to me.

"Don't lose this," he said. "You'll need it to go through customs in Sydney."

I pulled my pants up and boarded the plane, finding my designated seat. As I sat, I read the slip of paper, which said I had been examined by the US Army doctor, who found no visible signs of venereal disease.

I grinned at the GI taking the seat next to me.

"That doctor has to have one of the worst jobs in Vietnam," I said.

"He didn't look very happy," the GI said, grinning.

Once the plane was filled, the doors were closed, and it rumbled down the runway, lifting off over the South China Sea. The jetliner climbed sharply and banked to the right, headed south for Australia.

"No snipers down there," I said, looking down at the ocean.

"Nope," the GI said as he settled back into his seat. As the jetliner continued to climb, a strange silence filled the plane. There was no outburst of laughter or animated talk like you usually heard in a group of GIs. I wondered if the silence was because we had all been through an unusual public examination before boarding.

Still, I didn't feel any particular shame standing half naked on the tarmac, and I suspected other troops didn't either. After all, we were in the army, and we were accustomed to public exposure. We shared our barracks, tents, latrines, and mess halls. The army provided almost no privacy for anyone, including during medical examinations before flying to Australia.

Perhaps most important, however, was an unspoken understanding by everyone on the plane. We all knew that if we hadn't dropped our pants and showed our penises to the doctor, we would not be seated on this jetliner en route to Australia.

The jetliner flew south for several hours over the South China Sea before crossing over Borneo. Towering mountains rose up beneath us, giant peaks covered by thick jungle, even at the highest points. I could see numerous rivers and several giant waterfalls. The land looked devoid of people. There were no towns or villages and no visible roads.

After crossing over Borneo, the jetliner flew over the ocean again, but as nightfall approached we began passing over the scattered islands of Indonesia. Shortly after midnight, the jetliner landed at Darwin, on the northern tip of Australia. The plane was refueled, and we lifted off for the final leg of our journey to Sydney.

It was early morning when our flight began its final descent to Sydney Airport.

Once inside the terminal, we went through customs, where we each underwent a body search, and then the contents in our duffel bags were dumped onto tables. The Australians searched everything. They wanted to make sure we weren't bringing illegal drugs into their country.

Once we passed through customs, we boarded buses and were taken to the R&R headquarters in downtown Sydney. Everything was highly organized at the center, with racks of civilian clothes available for rent and lockers to store our military clothing.

After storing our army clothes and outfitting ourselves with civilian clothing, we began wandering out of the R&R center onto the streets of downtown Sydney. The city looked much like any American city except that the traffic flowed on the "other" side of the street. I soon found myself walking alone, away from the groups of GIs lingering outside the R&R center. It felt good to be away from others. It felt good to be wearing civilian clothing and walking alone on a street in Sydney, Australia.

After strolling several blocks, I spotted the Gladstone, a small hotel on a corner facing a small park. I went inside and booked a room for the week. My hotel room was perfect. It was quiet, with a comfortable bed and soft sheets. As soon as the bellboy left my room, I laid down on the bed, stretching my legs. I hadn't felt this comfortable in months. It was hard to believe I was in Sydney, free to go wherever I wanted without an M16 hanging from my shoulder. There would be no mortars falling in the night and no rifle at the foot of my bed. No war for one week.

In the days that followed, I explored Sydney, strolling through the downtown parks, watching an occasional movie and finding an interesting café for lunch.

One day, I rode an elevator to the top of Sydney's tallest building to look out over the sprawling city. Sydney stretched for miles beyond the harbor. A guide approached me as I stood at the railing. "You're looking down at one quarter of Australia's population," he said. Then he pointed out places of interest, including the unfinished Sydney Opera House on the edge of the harbor. "The construction process has been stalled for a bit," he said with a thin smile. Then he pointed to Hyde Park, acres of subtropical greenery bordering downtown Sydney.

The following day, I walked through the open construction gates and into the unfinished Sydney Opera House. Work had obviously been stopped for some time, as weeds were growing up through the cracks in the concrete floor, and flocks of birds were nesting high above on perches near the roof. I stood alone, staring up at the cavernous building. The immense shell made me feel small, insignificant, and lonely.

My nights in Sydney were mostly spent in the downtown bars and clubs. On my fifth night in Sydney, I met a young woman named Tasy Wilkes. She was slim with long brown hair and a warm smile. I loved listening to her speak with her thick Australian accent.

"You have an unusual first name," I said.

"I'm originally from Tasmania," she explained. "So that's how I got the nickname. My real name is Tamara, but everyone calls me Tasy."

On my last night on R&R, Tasy and I had dinner at a

club in downtown Sydney. It was a bittersweet moment. I felt good sitting across the table from this attractive girl. But I also knew that my Australian R&R would end in the morning. I dreaded returning to Vietnam.

After dinner, we went barhopping, stopping at several places to dance or just talk. As the night wore on, I drank heavily. Much later that night, we finally left the clubs and went to Tasy's flat.

"I have to be at the R&R center by 8 a.m.," I said as we undressed.

"Don't worry," she said. "I'll set the alarm for 6 a.m."

We went to bed and made love, and I quickly fell into a deep sleep, sedated by too much alcohol. I awakened the next morning with a headache, squinting my eyes at the bright sunshine flowing through the bedroom window.

Then I glanced down at the clock, which showed 8:10 a.m.

"Shit!" I screamed. "What happened to the alarm?"

"I don't know, I thought I had set it for 6 a.m.," Tasy said.

I jumped out of bed and quickly dressed while Tasy called for a cab. We embraced for one last kiss, and I rushed out the door and down the steps, just as the cab was pulling up to the curb.

"The R&R office at King's Cross Hotel," I told the driver. "I'm late, so step on it please."

Fifteen minutes later, the cab pulled up to the hotel. I paid the driver and ran into the building, the sounds of my feet pounding the floor echoing through the lobby. The R&R office was almost empty. An army sergeant was sitting behind the transit desk, staring at me.

"Goddamn alarm didn't go off," I said as I approached the desk.

"Well, you missed your flight," he said.

I stood back from his desk, turned, and shook my head in disgust. "Oh for Christ's sake, what do I do now?"

The sergeant picked up the passenger list for the flight.

"What's your name?'

"Alan Quale, Fourth Battalion, 11th Brigade."

The sergeant found my name and crossed it off on the list. Then he stared at me.

"I guess I'm in deep shit here," I said. "I'm fucking AWOL!"

The sergeant slid the passenger list to the side of his desk and folded his hands together.

"I'll try to get you on tomorrow's flight," he said.

"How can you do that?" I asked. "Aren't the flights always filled?"

He shook his head no. "The arriving flights are always filled, but there's almost always someone who misses their departing flight — someone like you. Actually, there were two of you who missed today's departure: you and an army captain we found drunk and wandering in a downtown park."

The sergeant grinned, but I couldn't find anything funny about my predicament. "Don't worry," he said. "There are always one or two guys who miss the flight, so I'm sure there will be room for you tomorrow. And when you get back to Vietnam, you'll still have to find your own way back to your base camp, but you know how to get around the country, right?"

I nodded yes, but my stomach was growing tight, and I felt like I might throw up at any moment.

"Get a hotel room as close to this office as possible," the sergeant continued. "And make sure you instruct the hotel desk to give you wake-up call. Be here tomorrow by 7 a.m., and I'll get you on the plane. And don't worry, we won't send a notice to your company in Vietnam saying you missed your flight."

His faced turned somber. "And one last thing: don't tell anyone that we got you on the next day's flight. If word gets out that we're doing this, everyone will be showing up late."

"I understand," I said. I turned and walked out of the R&R office, crossed the street, and booked a room in the Hampton Hotel for the night.

An unfriendly bellboy led me to the hotel elevator. As the elevator began to climb, he cast a scornful look at me.

We arrived at my room, I gave him a small tip, and he turned and left. I walked into the bathroom and examined myself in the mirror. My shirt had a wine stain on the front, my face was unshaved, and my eyes were bloodshot. I looked like a drunken bum. I could also see the worried look on my face. I was AWOL (absent without leave), one the worst offenses in the army.

*What a mess you've put yourself in. What a fucking dumb shit...*

I walked to the bed and sat on the edge, leaned forward, and held my head in my hands. I had never felt so alone in my life, stranded in Sydney, Australia, when I should have been seated on a jetliner, flying back to Vietnam. My face felt twisted and tight, my head throbbed, and there was a gnawing, unsettled feeling in my stomach.

My careless, stupid behavior on R&R changed everything. I knew my chances of surviving the Vietnam War were now directly connected to my actions in Sydney. I was AWOL, and the army was sure to punish me when I returned. I could be demoted in rank and removed as company supply sergeant. Then I likely would be sent to the field as an infantryman. My new job would be to continuously search for Charlie — to kill or be killed.

I had seen this punishment handed out before. Corporal Jeff Norstrom had been a company armorer who worked with me in base camp. He repaired rifles, grenade launchers, mortars, and other armaments when they were damaged or broken. Almost every day, I loaded a package of repaired arms onto the supply helicopter. Unbeknown to me, Corporal Norstrom was occasionally sending small amounts of marijuana to his friends in the field. The marijuana was hidden inside the barrels of rifles or inside other armaments. One day, a small bag of marijuana spilled out of the barrel of a grenade launcher soon after the weapon was delivered to the field. Captain Lewis saw the bag fall to the ground and picked it up.

The captain poured the leafy green contents into his hand. "What the fuck is this?" he asked a lieutenant who was standing nearby.

"Looks like marijuana," the lieutenant replied.

The captain ordered Norstrom to the field and launched an investigation. He soon learned that no one but Norstrom knew that he was sending the marijuana.

"Why did you do that?" the captain demanded.

"I did it for the guys in the field," Norstrom answered.

"Did you do it to make money?" the captain shouted.

"No sir," Norstrom said.

Captain Lewis demoted Norstrom to private, removed him as company armorer, and assigned him as a rifleman in the field. The incident reminded me of those scenes from old war movies in which a soldier does something wrong and is punished by being sent to the "front." The only difference between previous wars and the Vietnam

War was that the "front" was now called the "field." No matter what you called it, the army was still using the same tactic for punishment.

Now I sat on the edge of the hotel bed in Australia with my thoughts, nursing a hangover, with the nagging reminder that at that very moment, I was supposed to be seated on a jetliner. I slowly shook my head. There was no one else to blame for my predicament; it was my fault, and I would pay the consequences.

I spent a sleepless night in the hotel room and arrived early the next morning at the R&R office. Standing in line with the other GIs, we shuffled forward to a table where we would be given our boarding passes. My stomach tightened as I noticed that the sergeant at the table was a different man than the one I talked to the day before. I reached the front of the line.

"Name?" the sergeant asked.

"Sergeant Alan Quale, B Company, Fourth Battalion, 11th Brigade. I'm probably marked as standby."

He scanned a list of names on a sheet of paper but said nothing. Then he turned the paper over and began scanning more names on the back. Finally, he looked at a separate sheet of paper and nodded.

"Here you are. Quale, B Company, Fourth Battalion. You're in luck; we've got a seat for you today." He wrote my name on a boarding pass and handed it to me.

"Thank you," I said.

After receiving our boarding passes, we were ushered to the R&R locker room to retrieve our military fatigues and turn in our civilian clothes. After changing clothes, we went outside and began boarding buses. A crowd of Australians, probably going to work, paused to watch us climb onto the buses. Many in our group now wore camouflaged jungle fatigues, while others wore olive drab or brown fatigues. Our clothing said we didn't belong in Sydney; we were out of place, intruders once again in a foreign land.

The buses took us to the Sydney Airport where we were quickly processed through customs. We began boarding the jetliner, and a short while later, the plane roared down the runway and lifted off.

As the plane gained altitude, the captain came on the intercom. "Welcome aboard, gentlemen. I hope you had a good R&R in Sydney. Our flight time today will be nine hours. We'll arrive in Saigon at 8 p.m. local time."

*Son of a bitch! I thought we were going to Da Nang! Why didn't the R&R office tell me the flight was to Saigon?*

My eyes widened as I glanced around the plane at the other soldiers. No one seemed surprised, and why should they be? They had all processed out of Vietnam through Saigon, and now they were on their way back to Saigon.

My mind was racing as I tried to remember details of Vietnam's geography. I knew that Chu Lai was about 500 miles north of Saigon, and Duc Pho was about 50 miles south of Chu Lai, which meant that when we landed in Saigon, I'd still be more than 400 miles from my home base.

My relief at boarding the R&R flight out of Sydney was suddenly crushed, and my stomach was growing tighter again.

*I'm not going to make it in time. By the time I get back to base, several days will have passed, and the captain will know I missed my flight. And then the he'll get pissed off. He'll demote me and send me to the field, just like he did with Norstrom.*

I settled back in my seat, staring blankly at the ceiling. I tried to think of other things, but the same thought came racing back to my mind over and over again.

*I'm not going to make it.*

It was early evening when our plane descended over Saigon, landing at Tan Son Nhut Air Base. Once we disembarked, I found my way through the terminal to the standby transportation desk.

"I need to get to Landing Zone Bronco as soon as possible," I said.

"Where the fuck is Landing Zone Bronco?" asked the air force man behind the desk.

"About 50 miles south of Chu Lai," I answered. "It's next to Duc Pho."

He slid a binder from the side of his desk and opened it, scanning the flights that were penciled on the pages.

Finally his index finger stopped on a listing, and he looked up at me.

"There's nothing tonight, of course, but I have a flight going to Chu Lai tomorrow morning at 0800," he said. "I can give you a spot on that. Then you'll have to find your own way from Chu Lai to Landing Zone Bronco."

"Thanks," I said.

He handed me a boarding pass. "You can find a bunk for tonight in Barracks D." He motioned toward the doorway on the opposite side of the terminal. "When you go outside, cross the road, and you'll see Barracks D to the right."

I thanked the air force man again and walked out of the building. The following morning, I was first in line to board the flight on a C130 cargo plane to Chu Lai. The cargo plane accelerated down the runway and lifted off. I looked out the window at Saigon, its crowded streets lined by low white buildings that stretched for miles. As the city faded from view, I settled back into the netted seat on the side of the cargo plane.

*Once we land in Chu Lai, I should be able to catch a ride on a helicopter to Duc Pho. I'll make it back to camp by noon if everything goes right.*

There was always hope. I glanced out the small window on the side of the plane at the dark green rice paddies far below. The fields were slowly sliding by, a reassuring sight. The plane was steadily flying north toward Chu Lai, bringing me closer to my destination, perhaps saving me from being AWOL.

I knew that after landing in Chu Lai, the key to my success would be to find a helicopter destined to fly to Duc Pho as soon as possible.

I also began rehearsing how I would act when I returned to base camp. I would brag about my sexual conquests in Sydney, like everyone else did. I would act as though nothing out of the ordinary had happened. And I would resume work as the supply sergeant.

The cargo plane flew north for more than two hours and began a long descent to Chu Lai. Waves were crashing onto the white-sand beach as we crossed over and landed on the runway. I quickly got off the plane and headed toward several helicopters on a nearly landing pad. I soon found a helicopter preparing to transport a group of soldiers to Landing Zone Bronco. I recognized the pilots; they'd flown my supply helicopter over Pinkville one afternoon when we'd drawn gunfire from the ground.

I leaned into the doorway, "Can I hitch a ride to Duc Pho?"

"We've got some troops, so we're tight for room," one of the pilots said. "But I guess we can squeeze you in."

"Thanks," I said as I climbed on board. I found a place to sit between two soldiers. One of the pilots turned and stared at me as though he recognized me.

"Viet Cong still shooting at you over Pinkville?" I asked.

"Nope," he said, grinning. "We haven't been back to Pinkville. We want to stay away from there. It's like flying over a fucking hornet's nest out there; you never know what's going to come up and sting you in the ass."

The pilots laughed, and the helicopter's blades slowly began to rotate. As I settled into my seat, I noticed the other soldiers were staring at me. They'd been listening to our conversation.

"Don't worry," I said. "We're not going to fly over Pinkville today."

The soldiers said nothing. They just kept staring at me. They wore fresh jungle fatigues, and their boots were almost shiny. They'd probably finished boot camp weeks earlier. And now they were in a war zone halfway around the world. Some might even be replacements assigned to B Company. They kept staring. I knew they had questions, but I wasn't in the mood for talking. I was still worried about what would happen when I returned to base camp. Also, the anonymity of the army allowed me to ignore the soldiers. I turned my head to the side, leaned my face into netted seat, and closed my eyes for a nap.

I awakened as the helicopter swooped down, crossing the rice paddies and landing on the battered airstrip at Landing Zone Bronco. An army truck was waiting to pick up the soldiers, but I jumped out of the helicopter and walked past the soldiers, swinging my duffel bag over my shoulder and jogging toward the far side of camp. It looked like my plan was working.

Harris was the first to see me as I neared my tent.

"How was R&R?" he asked.

"It was great. I really liked Australia. The girls were beautiful and friendly too."

Harris looked tired. He had worked as supply sergeant while I was gone, along with his regular duties. "Everything go okay with your flights?" he asked. I thought I saw a suspicious look on Harris' face, but I wasn't sure.

"Yeah, everything went okay," I said. "But I had some problems finding a ride back here from Da Nang." It was the only time I had lied to Harris, and I could feel my face blush. "Anything happen here while I was gone?" I asked, anxious to change the subject.

"Charlie broke through our perimeter three nights ago, down by D Company's sector," Harris replied. "It was mostly a bunch of sappers making their way into camp and throwing their satchel charges into tents and bunkers. No one knew what was happening, and since most of the men in D Company are new here, they got confused and started shooting at each another. It was a fucking mess."

"What were the casualties?" I asked.

"Two killed and eleven wounded," Harris said. "Not as bad as it could have been, but it's scary when they break through the perimeter." Harris shook his head and turned to walk away. "I'm too short for this shit."

I walked to my supply tent and went inside, setting my duffel bag on the floor. Then I went outside, lit a cigarette, and leaned back against the sandbag wall, exhaling the smoke. My plan appeared to be working, at least so far.

Five days later, I was loading supplies into my jeep when Sergeant Tony Padilla from Headquarters Company approached. As he got closer, I noticed that he was holding a piece of paper in his right hand.

"Hey, Quale, I thought you might be interested in seeing this," he said, handing the paper to me.

The letterhead at the top said "R&R Office, Sydney, Australia." My heart began to pound as I started reading the text.

"This is to inform you that Sergeant Alan Quale, E-5 was a no-show for his scheduled flight out of Sydney Airport on 3 May 1968," the letter began.

My mouth dropped open. "Those fuckers! They said they weren't going to report me!"

I looked up at Sergeant Padilla, searching for clues. A thin, enigmatic smile was forming on his face. "I thought you might want to keep this letter," he said. "It's the only one we have."

"Yes, I'd like that," I said. "Thanks."

Sergeant Padilla handed the letter to me and began walking away, and then he stopped and turned to face me again. "How was R&R?" He had a big smile now; his teeth were showing.

"It was great," I said. "But time went by fast. Before I

knew it, R&R was over."

"Yeah, that's obvious," Sergeant Padilla said as he laughed and waved good-bye.

I went into my tent, found my Zippo lighter, and walked out the back door. I glanced in all directions, and when I saw no one, I set the letter on fire. The flames crawled up the middle of the letter, and I dropped it in the dirt, watching the fire consume the entire page. When it was completely burned, I stepped on it, grinding the ashes into the ground.

I went back inside my tent and sat on my cot. I felt like the condemned man who was spared from hanging at the last moment. Now I knew I would not be punished for being AWOL. I was relieved and very happy. *How can I be so fucking lucky?*

My good luck might have been tied to the Viet Cong sapper assault on Landing Zone Bronco. For several days after the attack, the officers at Headquarters Company were called away from their regular duties to supervise repairs to the battered bunkers on the perimeter. They probably did not read all of their correspondence, including a letter from the R&R office in Sydney, so that duty fell to Sergeant Padilla, and he was a friend of mine.

I stepped outside my tent, looking at the distant mountains. White cumulus clouds were forming above the higher peaks, a sharp contrast to the dark-green slopes below. It was a beautiful, calm sight, which seemed strangely befitting.

17 May 1968
Back from R&R

Dear Mom and Dad,

I was lucky to get out of Vietnam for R&R because the Viet Cong threw 40 rockets into Da Nang the night before we were scheduled to leave. Fortunately, none of the rockets struck our plane, which was parked at the runway.

Australia was one of the nicest places I've ever visited. The people were friendly, and the girls were beautiful. Sydney, although a very large city, is quite clean and possibly a little more European than US cities. The beaches are really nice, although it's cool "winter" weather down there right now. When I left Sydney, I flew to Saigon and stayed at Ton San Nhut. Then I made my way by cargo plane and helicopter back here to Duc Pho.

Things here are pretty much the same, but when I was gone, the Viet Cong attacked our base camp, but they were eventually beaten back. I'm hoping it was one of their last big offensives here because of the ongoing peace talks being held in Paris.

Well, it's late, so I better sign off. Keep the letters coming.

Your son,
Alan

*Alan Quale*

21 May 1968

Dear Carol and Wally,

I'm on bunker guard, and since the sun hasn't set, I'm sitting on some sandbags outside the bunker in the rain as I write this. It's very hot, so I don't mind the moisture.

I've got approximately 70 days until I leave this place, and I can hardly wait. A normal ETS (end of time in service) is nice, but when you ETS out of Vietnam, it's twice as nice. I don't know what I'll do when I get out of the army. I'll have to think of doing something other than wearing green clothes and carrying a gun. I'll probably be a bum for a while, taking life easy.

The recent peace talks in Paris haven't affected anything here except probably increase the fighting. Ironic, isn't it?

Australia was really nice. I was having such a good time there that I was one day tardy in leaving. I missed my 8 a.m. flight, but the R&R folks agreed to let me fly standby the following day. So the next day, I flew from Sydney to Darwin, where we refueled, and then on to Saigon. From Saigon, I flew on a cargo plane to Chu Lai, and then I caught a ride on a helicopter to Duc Pho. I should have my wings pretty soon.

*Well, Australia is long gone now—I have just the memories. It was really a nice break. I think I might try to get back there again some day.*

> *70 days to go,*
> *Alan*

*PS. (The next day) Last night, our bunker drew some sniper fire from Charlie, so I fired some grenades in front of my bunker with the grenade launcher. Now the soldiers in the tents behind our bunker say we filled their tents full of shrapnel. Sorry bastards! I think the only thing that hit their tents was mud from the explosions.*

# Chapter 10
# My Replacement

I was loading supplies into my jeep when Captain Lewis called me on the radio. "I want you to come out and spend some time with us in the field," he said. "Talk to the troops about their supply issues. You and I can also discuss the resupply schedules to see if any changes are needed."

There was a pause on the radio before Captain Lewis continued speaking. "And we need to talk about your replacement."

"Yes sir," I said, trying to hide my excitement. It was the first time anyone in the army had said "your replacement" to me.

"I've chosen Sergeant Mike Sundvor," the captain continued. "He'll be coming in soon, and you can train him to take over when you leave."

"Yes sir," I said. "When do you want me to come out to the field?"

"As soon as possible," the captain said.

"I'll be there on the resupply copter tomorrow." I laid the radio transmitter on the table, walked out of my tent, and lit a cigarette. The morning was hot and muggy, and the cigarette smoke lingered in the air.

"Replacement," I said as I exhaled more smoke. Suddenly the word had a different meaning. *Replacement* was no longer associated with death, identifying mutilated bodies, or inventorying personal belongings. *Replacement* meant I would be going home soon.

I went into my tent and readied my pack to take to the field. I wasn't sure how long I would be gone, but I suspected it wouldn't be long. To be effective, a supply sergeant had to be near his supply source. I once went to the field and stayed with the company for three days. On the second day, everything unraveled as the supply helicopter arrived late, and several requested supplies were missing. Captain Lewis shook his head and turned to me. "You'd better get back to base camp and straighten that shit out."

Now I was headed back out to the field, likely for the last time. I had mixed feelings about this trip; I felt good, knowing it would be my last extended trip to the field, but I also felt a sense of danger since the company was now patrolling in the middle of Pinkville. And while my anxiety grew, I was sure that Sergeant Sundvor was feeling a sense of relief that he soon would be leaving the field.

Sergeant Sundvor had a serious, almost formal demeanor, especially for the army and especially in a place like Vietnam. He always addressed me as "Sergeant Quale," which made me feel slightly uncomfortable. Sundvor also had a reserved appearance. He was tall, with a crew cut and a thin mustache, and his jungle fatigues always looked less soiled than the fatigues worn by other men. He was the leader of a rifle squad, and his men respected him.

I was surprised that Captain Lewis chose Sundvor to replace me, because Sundvor was becoming "short" with only five months left in his Vietnam tour. But the more I thought about it, the more it looked like Captain Lewis was doing a favor for his most trusted squad leader. By removing Sundvor from the field and sending him to work in base camp, the captain was increasing Sundvor's chances of surviving the Vietnam War.

The following day, I was the only passenger as the helicopter lifted off from base camp and flew north toward Pinkville. I looked down at the green rice fields and the villages with their clusters of yellow and gray huts. From the helicopter, the countryside looked peaceful, almost picturesque, but on the ground below, I knew it was a far different story.

Soon the helicopter approached a large hill. Near the top were the bunkers and tents of Fire Base Betty. The helicopter circled the hill once, and a smoke flare appeared on the far side, signaling that we should land there. After the helicopter landed, I jumped out and started unloading supplies.

"Hey, Sergeant Quale. Glad you made it out."

I turned to see Captain Lewis approach.

"Yes sir," I said. "I like your camp way up here on top of the hill."

"Charlie is going to have to do a lot of climbing if he wants to get us," the captain said. "I'll catch up with you later." He began walking in the opposite direction.

Two soldiers approached and helped me unload the remaining supplies. Once the helicopter was empty, the pilots looked out the window and motioned for me to get on board.

I waved them off and mouthed the words, "I'm staying here." The pilots nodded, and the helicopter lifted up and flew away.

I stood next to the supplies, looking down the hill at the dark green rice fields and the small villages scattered throughout the plain. Everything looked so tranquil, but I knew I was looking down at a land filled with violence, a place where the killing never stopped. I had been warned about Pinkville by infantrymen. They said the trails were especially dangerous because they were lined with mines and booby traps. The villagers seemed to instinctively know where the explosives were buried, but the Americans did not. After several casualties, the American troops abandoned the pathways altogether. Still, no place was safe for Americans in Pinkville, a place where so many men from B Company had fallen dead or wounded.

The next morning, a group of infantrymen descended from the hilltop to patrol through nearby villages, a routine that would be repeated each day by rotating groups.

On my second day at the firebase, I joined the third platoon on patrol. Captain Lewis wanted me to experience life in the field, albeit briefly, to make me more aware of the supply needs of the infantrymen. Shortly after sunrise, we put on our gear and began moving down the hillside.

"Spread out," ordered Lieutenant Marvin Hatch, the platoon leader. "And stay off the goddamn trails." Hatch was a tall, slim man who towered above everyone else, which seemed to increase his authority.

The infantrymen began extending the distance between one another until most of men were at least 20 feet apart. The added space would reduce the number of casualties should someone step on a mine, and it also created a more scattered target for snipers.

We descended the hill through waist-high grass before reaching the rice paddies. The point man paused for a second before stepping into the rice paddy, and the line of troops followed into the ankle-deep water.

My boots were immediately waterlogged as we plodded forward, producing a monotonous sloshing sound under the hot, cloudless sky. I looked at the fields, but there were no farmers anywhere—only our long, extended column of infantrymen. The land was silent except for the sloshing as we moved forward.

One hour later, we approached a village of low-thatched huts clustered on an embankment a few feet above the water. Lieutenant Hatch raised his hand, a signal for us to stop. Everyone stood still, listening, looking for movement, but the village appeared deserted. The huts seemed to sag in the hot, muggy air, and the silence was unsettling. Finally, Lieutenant Hatch signaled for us to move forward. The infantrymen advanced slowly, swinging their heads to the left and right, searching for any movement. At the front of the column, the point man climbed up the embankment and moved into the village.

The line of troops followed into the village, stopping occasionally as infantrymen searched huts. Everything was done in sequence, and soon it was my turn.

"Quale, search the hooch on the right." Lieutenant Hatch shouted back to me.

"Okay," I hollered. "I'm going now."

The hut was dilapidated, its walls bleached white by the sun and the sagging roof barely visible above the outside walls.

I slowly pulled back the cloth that covered the door, searching the frame for wires or string before stepping inside. The air inside was warm with a strange odor. Sweat began dripping down from my forehead as I began my search. I pointed my M16 at a large thatched basket, using the end of the barrel to lift a blanket off the top. It was empty.

In the center of the hut was a fire pit with a small pot in the middle. I knelt down and felt the side of the pot, which was warm to touch. I stood and turned, almost expecting to see someone standing there, but there was no one. I examined some pottery in a cabinet and patted clothing lying on a cot, feeling for hard objects. There were no weapons or suspicious objects anywhere.

I stepped outside, shielding my eyes from the bright sun. "I found nothing, except a warm pot in the fire pit," I shouted to Lieutenant Hatch. "Someone was in this hut not long ago."

Lieutenant Hatch nodded and motioned for the platoon to move forward. Soon we neared a well in the center of the village. Lieutenant Hatch stopped, peered down into the well, and then motioned for us to continue. We reached the far side of the village and followed the point man down a bank into another rice paddy.

By midday, we climbed out of the water and up onto a low embankment and into a grove of trees. I could see the tall hill in the far distance where Fire Base Betty was located.

"We'll stop here for lunch," Hatch shouted. "Keep your eyes open, and stay alert. It's too goddamn quiet here, I don't like this shit." Hatch said what everyone was thinking. It seemed like we were patrolling a no-man's-land with the empty fields and deserted villages. Nothing looked normal. There was only the strange calm under the hot sun.

After eating our C rations, we sat on the ground, smoking cigarettes and talking. "I guess you'd rather be back in base camp?" asked Corporal Ed Martinez. His voice had a taunting tone.

"Beats the shit out of this," I said. "Although today doesn't seem that bad." I paused for a moment. "But then what do I know? I'm a REMF."

Martinez laughed loudly and took a long drink from his canteen. I knew I had said the right words, the words he was thinking.

"All right, let's move out," shouted Lieutenant Hatch. Everyone stood and straightened their gear, and one by one, we stepped back into the rice paddy, spreading the distance between us until we were once again a long line of troops sloshing through the water. By midafternoon, we approached a second village, which sat on a low embankment, only feet above the rice paddy water. The lieutenant signaled for us to stop, and everyone stood still, listening and slowly moving their heads to the left and right. I sensed this was a highly organized platoon; the infantrymen were meticulous in their movements. The point man climbed up the bank to enter the village, and the line of infantrymen followed.

"I don't like this shit at all," said Corporal Vince Lowell, the man 20 feet in front of me. He was talking to me over his shoulder. "Nothing looks right, so keep your eyes open."

I nodded and followed, climbing up the dike. The huts were scattered haphazardly. A pig suddenly darted out from the side of a hut, squealed, and ran the opposite direction. Corporal Lowell aimed his M16 at the fleeing pig, but he didn't fire. We continued moving forward, stopping as squad members searched some of the huts.

Suddenly there was a single gunshot near the front of our column. We dropped to the ground and heard troops shouting ahead of us, but we couldn't see what was happening because the huts blocked our view. Moments later, word was passed down the line that a woman had been shot dead.

We stood and began moving forward. As we neared the center of the village, Lieutenant Hatch was knelt over the dead woman, searching her body for weapons. Her arms extended from her sides, and her straw cone lay nearby. As we neared the area, the lieutenant stood and walked away.

I heard a strange, whimpering sound. I stopped and turned my head to the left and right and lowered myself to a crouching position.

*Where the fuck is that coming from?*

I heard the sound again and discovered it was from Corporal Lowell. As he approached the dead woman, he dropped to his knees beside her and laid his rifle on the ground. He bent forward, wrapping his arms around her shoulders and pulling the lifeless woman up to his chest, hugging her.

"Mom," he sobbed. There were tears running down his face. I moved closer and stood beside him. "Mom," he repeated in a loud, mournful voice.

"That's not your mother," I said, my words sounding hard and cold.

"Mom!" Corporal Lowell repeated, ignoring my comment. "Mom!" he screamed. He laid the dead woman back on the ground and began moving away from her, walking on his knees. I picked up the corporal's rifle and followed him, not knowing what to do. Then he turned and began moving back toward the dead woman, still on his knees. His twisted face was still wet with tears as he bent over the woman and began brushing hair away from her face.

"It's not your mother," I repeated. "We have to move out." I motioned toward the troops who were waiting in front of us.

Corporal Lowell slowly stood facing me. He looked confused, like he didn't know where he was. He glanced at the troops waiting in front of us.

"We've got to go," one of troops shouted.

Lowell, however, was still trying to focus on his surroundings. He turned in a circle, looking at everything. Finally his eyes dropped again to the dead woman. His face hardened, and he turned toward me.

"She might not be my mother, but she looks like my mother!" he screamed. "What's the fucking difference?" He turned to follow the column.

I still held his M16, so I followed him, simultaneously flipping the safety switch on. After a few minutes, I caught up with Corporal Lowell, and he turned. The hard, angry look was gone, and he now appeared embarrassed.

"Here's your gun," I said, handing the weapon to him. He grabbed the weapon, turned, and began walking. I waited until he was 20 feet in front of me and followed. As we advanced through the village, I heard the strange whimpering sound again. I knew it was from Corporal Lowell.

Later that day, we completed our patrol, wading out of the rice paddies onto dry land at the base of the hill. A soft breeze swayed the tall green grass up the steep slopes. The hill looked inviting with our firebase at the top. As we climbed toward camp, word was passed down the line that the woman was shot by the point man when she darted out of a hut and began running away. I knew there would be no inquiry; the woman's death would simply be marked as "enemy killed." Indeed, she might have been the enemy, but we would never know.

It had been a strange day patrolling the silent, empty land, knowing there were likely eyes watching us from the distant groves of palm trees. A single shot was fired, a woman fell dead, and an American soldier collapsed in despair. There didn't seem to be any logic to our patrol.

On my third day in the camp, Captain Lewis and I were discussing supply issues, when two soldiers entered the captain's tent.

"Sir, we've captured three Viet Cong," one of the soldiers announced. "We saw them laying mines in a trail outside a village."

Captain Lewis' face instantly hardened, his lips drawn tight. "Where are they?" he asked.

"We got them over by the ammunitions bunker," the soldier answered.

The captain put on his helmet, grabbed his M16, and

rushed out of the tent. I dropped the pad of paper I was holding and followed.

As we approached, I saw the three Vietnamese standing rigidly next to the bunker, their arms bound tightly behind their backs.

The three prisoners all wore black pants and loose fitting, tan shirts. Their faces looked defiant and hard, but when Captain Lewis approached, I could see fear growing in their eyes.

Captain Lewis looked furious; his face was filled with hate. He stood in front of the prisoners, glaring at them and slowly reached into his pocket, pulling out a leather glove and sliding it onto his right hand.

Suddenly, he struck one of the prisoners squarely in the face. The prisoner staggered but remained standing, blood pouring out of his nose. Then the captain struck the prisoner again, this time producing a loud cracking noise. The prisoner fell backward to the ground, landing on his bound arms.

"You son of a bitches are going to tell me everything I need to know! Every goddamn thing!" the captain shouted. Two infantrymen stepped forward and pulled the fallen prisoner to his feet.

"Take these assholes away!" the captain bellowed. "I'll deal with them later."

The captain's face was flushed with anger as he turned toward me, pulling the bloody glove from his hand. "Now you know why I ordered this pair of leather gloves," he said.

I nodded but said nothing. My thoughts were of the prisoner; I almost felt sorry for him. He couldn't defend himself when the captain stepped forward, smashing his fist into his face. The prisoner didn't cry out in pain or shout in anger; he fell to the ground and lay there silently until he was pulled back up to his feet.

But there was something else about these prisoners. It was the first time I had seen Viet Cong up close. They were standing in front of me, no longer hidden by darkness. They looked innocent, much like the farmers who worked in the rice fields bordering base camp.

Two soldiers approached to take the prisoners away. I continued staring at the prisoners, wondering what would happen if the tables were turned, what if we were captured by them?

With the captain gone, the prisoners' faces were turning hard and defiant again, which answered my question. If these Viet Cong captured any of us, there would be no interrogation. There would only be a knife slicing deep across our throats, and we would be thrown to the ground to die. They would not lessen our pain with a single bullet to the head, because that would be too costly; they would save their ammunition for future attacks.

I turned to leave. The captain was far ahead of me, walking fast, his boots stomping the ground. I followed, my boots also landing hard on the dirt, my face growing tight with anger. I realized that I hated the prisoners as much as the captain did.

The following day, I gathered my things and prepared to leave on the supply helicopter. I slid the yellow pad with supply requests into my pack and walked with the captain to the area where the helicopter would land. The helicopter was late, and the sun was dropping lower above the mountains.

"I'll send Sergeant Sundvor into base camp next week so that you can start training him," Captain Lewis said.

"Yes sir."

The resupply helicopter suddenly appeared on the side of the hill, and as it drew closer, the captain raised his voice to be heard above the noise.

"Do you know why I chose Sergeant Sundvor?" the captain shouted.

"Yes sir, I think I do."

"He's a good man," the captain said, a thin smile on his face. "I know he'll be a good supply sergeant."

The helicopter landed, and two soldiers began unloading the supplies. I turned to help them, but the captain wasn't done talking to me.

"So we're in agreement on moving the resupply up one hour in the afternoon?" the captain shouted.

"Yes sir, I think that will be good."

The supplies were unloaded, but the captain continued talking. He motioned to the helicopter pilots to wait, even as they were increasing the helicopter's rotor speed, a signal they were anxious to lift off.

After a few minutes, the captain quit talking and was turning to leave, but then he stopped. "I almost forgot. I've got a letter I want you to mail to my wife when you get back to camp. I'll go get it."

The captain again motioned to the pilots to wait as he walked toward his tent. I turned to the pilots and shrugged my shoulders. They sat motionless, glaring at me. Five minutes passed. I looked at my watch and glanced at the captain's tent. I was worried the pilots might leave without me. Another five minutes passed, and the captain finally emerged from his tent. He walked to me, handing me the letter. "I couldn't remember where I put it," he shouted.

I nodded and moved quickly to the helicopter, climbing up through the open door. One of the pilots turned and gave me an irritated look. "Ready for takeoff, sergeant?" he shouted in a sarcastic voice.

I said nothing; I only nodded and pulled the safety strap down over my shoulder. I was annoyed with the pilots.

Relations between supply sergeants and helicopter pilots were often strained in Vietnam. Pilots complained that we overloaded their helicopters with supplies. Supply sergeants, in turn, accused pilots of tossing needed supplies from their helicopters at the last moment before liftoff.

Now, as the helicopter lifted up from Fire Base Betty, I sat alone in the empty cargo area, staring out the open door. I was surprised by the growing darkness, realizing why the pilots were so anxious to leave. Dusk was fast approaching, and no one wanted to fly over Pinkville at night. A blinking helicopter light in the sky was an easy target.

The helicopter banked to the right and flew down the hillside, dropping until we were only 100 feet above the rice paddies. Then we began flying at top speed toward Duc Pho, a fast-moving target, seen from the ground for only a few seconds as we passed overhead. In the fading light, I watched the fields and villages fly by, wondering which of the villages was home to the Viet Cong prisoners. *And now what will become of them?*

We continued south at top speed, passing only a few feet above the tallest trees. I saw the pilots move their levers, guiding their helicopter. They looked anxious, talking to each other via headsets in their helmets, but I couldn't hear what they were saying.

Suddenly there was an ear-cracking sound, and the helicopter shuddered. The helicopter plunged to only a few feet above the water. I looked out the door at the rice paddies flashing by and then at the pilots. They were shouting at each other as they moved their heads closer to the window. They were looking for something.

Suddenly the helicopter surged upward over a hedgerow, the treetops brushing the bottom of the helicopter. Then the helicopter dropped down again; we were only a few feet above the rice paddies. It seemed as though we were fleeing from something. The helicopter raced forward, surging up over approaching hedgerows and then dropping low again over rice paddies.

It was almost dark when we approached Landing Zone Bronco. A small group of lights was turned on alongside the airstrip to guide us in. The pilots lowered their helicopter to the ground and began turning switches to shut everything down. The rotor blades slowed and finally stopped. Both plots removed their helmets and turned toward me. They looked angry.

"That was a rocket you heard back there," one pilot said. "It passed no more than 50 feet from the copter."

"That's too fucking close for comfort!" the other pilot shouted. "Now you know why we don't like to fuck around, delaying our lift off from Fire Base Betty. The Viet Cong have caches of rockets all around Pinkville, just waiting for a target. Flying at dusk is too fucking dangerous out there. So you might want to tell your captain that."

I nodded my head. For the first time, I agreed with the helicopter pilots on something.

The following Wednesday, I stood next to my jeep at the helicopter landing pad, waiting for Sergeant Sundvor. Soon the helicopter appeared and began its descent. Sundvor jumped out of the copter, swung a bag over his shoulder and walked toward me. We shook hands, climbed in the jeep and drove to my supply tent.

In the days that followed, I guided my replacement through all the supply procedures. Sergeant Sundvor was a good student, taking the supply requests over the radio and assembling them in our tent for transport to the helicopter pad. I set up a cot at the rear of the tent, opposite my cot, where Sundvor could sleep.

On his fourth night in camp, Sundvor stared curiously at me as I went through my nightly routine, lining up my boots, helmet, M16, and ammunition on the floor.

"Do you think Charlie is going to attack tonight?" he asked.

"You never know," I said. "Mostly we get a lot of mortar here at night, so it's best to have your gear in place to make your way to a bunker. You want to get out of this tent as fast as possible."

Sergeant Sundvor nodded and laid his gear on the floor, much like mine.

We both settled into our cots and began talking about our future plans after the army. Sergeant Sundvor said he had two years of college and planned to return to school and earn a degree in police administration. He missed his wife, his two kids, and his parents, who lived down the road from his house in upstate New York.

"How about you?" he asked.

"I've got a degree in journalism, so I guess I should try working at a newspaper," I said. "But I'm not exactly sure what I'll do when I get out."

"How did you get in this mess? " Sundvor asked.

"I got my draft notice in the mail the same day I graduated from the University of North Dakota. Talk about a bittersweet day." I rolled sideways on my cot and tucked the mosquito net under my poncho liner. "How about you?"

"I enlisted for three years," Sundvor said. "You know how it goes. I was going to help save the world from the commies. The dumbest thing I've ever done in my life."

We both laughed, and Sundvor cleared his throat. "You know, Quale, there's some bad shit going on out there in the field."

It was the first time Sundvor dropped "sergeant" from my name; I lifted my head up from my cot, sensing that he had something important to tell me. "Yeah, I know," I said. "I saw Captain Lewis interrogate the Viet Cong prisoners. He smashed the fucking Viet Cong twice in the face, probably broke his nose. Who knows what he did later when he interrogated them."

"There's a lot worse things happening than that," Sundvor said.

"Like what?" I asked.

"You know Crestfield, the kid from Arkansas. One day, he stops this older man, a papa son who was riding a bicycle on the trail outside a village and asks for his papers. The papa son obliges, pulling a paper from his pocket. Crestfield examines it and nods yes, motioning for the papa son to go. 'Di di mau,' Crestfield says. So the old man climbs back on his bicycle and continues on his way. But then Crestfield raises his M16, takes aim, and shoots the old man in the back."

"That won't win a lot of converts in the village," I said, "except for the Viet Cong."

"And then there's Marley from the third platoon," Sundvor continued. "You know he's crazy as hell."

Yeah, I know. Completely zonkers."

"Marley shot a mama son outside her hut. She wasn't doing anything wrong; she was just standing there watching the troops enter her village. When Marley approached, he suddenly raised his M16 and fired one bullet through her head.

"Hubbard from second squad was really pissed, and he runs up to Marley and grabs him by the shoulders and shakes him. 'Why did you do that?' Hubbard screams. Marley didn't say anything; he just shrugs his shoulders."

"Where was the captain when all this shit was going on?" I asked.

"You know how it is in the field, with the company all spread out," Sundvor answered. "The old man probably didn't see a thing."

Sergeant Sundvor cleared his throat and swung his legs out of his cot and stood. I could see him in the dim light.

"And I did something *really* bad," he said in a hushed voice, speaking as though he didn't want anyone else to hear. He started pacing back and forth in front of his cot.

"What'd you do?" I asked.

"We were patrolling an area five klicks south of Hien Luong last month, and as we approached a village, we came under heavy fire. You remember, that was the day Corporal Jackson and Sergeant Calveras were both shot dead. And when Corporal Heggen ran for cover, he stepped on a mine and got his foot blown off. There were guys falling all around me, but somehow I didn't get hit." Sundvor paused, inhaling a long breath of air and then exhaling.

"The gunfire didn't last long, and soon we managed to make our way to the edge of the village. Captain Lewis ordered my squad to sweep through the village and search the hooches.

"We started searching but found nothing; there were no people or animals. But when we neared the far side of the village, we found three old men standing alongside the village well. We approached, guns drawn, and searched them, learning that the oldest of the three men was the village chief.

"I asked him where the Viet Cong had gone. 'No VC,' the chief said, shaking his head.

"At that point I was getting angry. 'Then who was shooting at us?' I shouted.

"The chief looked at me and repeated, 'No VC,' and he waved his hand as if to dismiss my question."

Sundvor paused and exhaled another long rush of air. "I was getting mad. I was losing control. I motioned to the other two villagers to leave the area. Then I screamed at the chief, 'You fucker! Where are the VC?' The chief shook his head and shrugged his shoulders.

"I slapped him hard across his face and shouted at him again: 'Two of our men are dead and three, wounded, and you say there are no VC!'

"The old man shrugged his shoulders again and repeated, 'No VC.' I moved closer to him, and it was then that I noticed his eyes. They were steely black and seemed filled with hatred."

Sundvor exhaled another long rush of air. It sounded like he was having difficulty breathing.

"And then, I don't know what happened. It felt like my whole body was being twisted into a tight knot. My hands started to shake. I dropped my M16 to the ground and drew my machete, pushing the chief to the ground. I stared straight into his steely eyes as I made the first slice across his throat. He began to gag, so I kept slicing. Then I raised my machete and started chopping at his neck."

Sundvor abruptly stopped talking. The only sound was his loud breathing as he paced back and forth in front of his cot.

"I chopped and chopped," said Sundvor, his voice turning high pitched and raspy. "I kept chopping and chopping," he sobbed.

"I chopped his head completely off. It rolled on the

ground. I picked the head up and took it to the well and dropped it into the water."

Sundvor stopped sobbing, and everything grew quiet. I waited for him to continue talking, but he said nothing.

"How could you do that?" I asked.

"I don't know," Sundvor said. "I have no fucking idea."

He lit a cigarette and exhaled loudly, blowing the smoke in my direction.

"When I was a boy, my dad used to take me squirrel hunting in upstate New York," he said. "I really didn't want to go, but I went anyway, just to make my dad happy."

I stared at Sundvor through the dim light, wondering why he suddenly changed the subject. *Is he going crazy?* My eyes dropped to my M16 to reassure myself, just in case.

"Why didn't you want to go squirrel hunting with your dad?" I asked.

"I felt sorry for the squirrels," he said. "Can you believe that? And now I've done this…"

Sundvor cleared his throat and then was silent. I knew he was waiting for a response, but I didn't know what to say. What do you say to man who confessed to murder? A killer who chops the head off a helpless old man?

I sat still on my cot, shocked and confused, searching for the right words. I reached into my shirt pocket and pulled out a cigarette, lighting it and blowing the smoke toward Sundvor. "You felt sorry for the squirrels, so hang on to that thought."

"Why?" Sundvor asked.

"You might need it when you get back to the world."

I heard Sundvor blowing his nose. It sounded like he was crying again, but I wasn't sure because of the dim light. Then he cleared his throat. "Thanks for listening," he said in a more normal voice. He stubbed his cigarette on the floor and dropped it in an ash can. I heard him crawling back onto his cot and pulling his poncho liner over him. It was quiet again in the tent. I could hear Sundvor breathing. His gasps for air were gone, and his breathing sounded almost normal. Soon he began snoring softly.

I stubbed my cigarette on the floor, put it in an ash can, and lay on my back on my cot, staring up through the open flap at the top of the tent. The stars were bright and sparkling in the night sky. Everything looked so serene. But I knew I was looking at only half of the picture. Below those dazzling stars, a brutal war continued. At that moment, I was sure that people were being slaughtered somewhere in Vietnam. The night sky was nothing more than a cruel illusion.

*The heaven above – the hell below.*

I couldn't sleep. For a moment, I even considered going outside and climbing up on the roof of the tent and closing the flap. But I knew that blocking out the view of the night sky wouldn't do any good; the stars would still be up there, continuing their heavenly orbits, no matter what we did on earth. I closed my eyes and tried to think of pleasant thoughts of home, but it was of no use. There was only the stark image of Sergeant Sundvor slicing and hacking at the old man's throat and the sound of the severed head splashing into the well water.

10 June 1968
Duc Pho

Dear Mom and Dad,

There's been quite a lot happening here lately. Our company commander was transferred to S-2 (everyone called him Mad Dog behind his back). But I kind of miss the cranky captain, because he was always good to me, promoting me to supply sergeant and everything. When I look back at the time I worked for him, he treated me fairly, although we had our arguments regarding supplies.

He told me he put me in for a Bronze Star for Achievement, but I'll never get it (not a chance in hell). I think he did it mainly to show some sort of thanks for working for him all those months.

Our new commanding officer, Captain Robert Hershell, seems squared away. He came into my tent and introduced himself and shook my hand. Officers usually don't do that. He's also a short timer and leaves Vietnam in October.

Well, it's getting late, so I'd better sign off. Sorry if I've been a little slow at writing, but it's the same old story here, busy as hell. Anyway, I don't want you to worry about me if my letters are a little slow to arrive at your house.

You know I'm going to take care of myself over here. I'll be home soon. My tent is like an iron fortress with tall walls of sandbags surrounding it. There are lots of guys over here, especially those out in the field, who have it much worse than me.

Your son,
Alan

# Chapter 11

# As Different as Night and Day

As summer approached, the Viet Cong increased their attacks on Landing Zone Bronco. Firefights erupted almost every night on the base perimeter, and the mortar attacks were more frequent. It seemed as though the Viet Cong were making a final attempt to overrun our base camp at the foot of the big hill.

The Viet Cong also changed their tactics by setting up their mortar tubes *inside* Duc Pho, knowing the Americans were less likely to return mortar fire or call in artillery against the VC in a "friendly" village.

"I don't care what the military brass thinks. We ought to blow that fucking village off the map," Sergeant Sundvor said. "Everyone in Duc Pho hates us, so why not return the favor?" Although many American troops agreed with Sundvor, Duc Pho was still a hard place to define. Certainly there were the hard looks on the villagers' faces when we visited the marketplace, but we had no idea what expressions the villagers showed the Viet Cong when they encountered them.

In many ways, Duc Pho was an enigma. It was like two very different villages. During the day, everything looked normal. The marketplace was filled with shoppers.

Orphans sold marijuana outside the fading white walls of the orphanage. Vietnamese rode their bicycles and motorbikes through the verdant groves of palm trees and into the village on Highway 1.

At night, Duc Pho became a different, dangerous place where one could easily be killed. The village was supposedly under the control of the Vietnamese army, but as darkness approached, the ARVN troops retreated to their huge cinder-block bunker in the middle of Duc Pho. On the bunker's roof, the ARVNs turned on giant spotlights, slowly panning the beams on adjacent roadways. After sunset, the Vietnamese troops shot at anything that moved, occasionally killing a wandering pig or water buffalo. In the morning, the ARVN soldiers would emerge from the bunker and nod their heads approvingly, looking past the occasional dead livestock — they had held Duc Pho for another night.

The ARVNs, however, controlled only their bunker. The rest of Duc Pho was free range for the Viet Cong, who moved easily through the nighttime shadows, ignoring the ARVNs holed up inside their bunker. As darkness fell, the Viet Cong began setting up their mortar tubes, aiming at Landing Zone Bronco. As the mortar attacks began, villagers huddled inside their huts, not knowing what would happen next. Would the Americans unleash their mortar on the village, or, even worse, would they call in artillery? No one knew the answer, but the villagers would not plead with the Viet Cong to stop their attacks. They knew that complaining to the Viet Cong might be even more dangerous than risking an attack from the

Americans.

The Americans did not strike back, even as the mortar attacks continued from the village. Finally, after several nights, the Viet Cong stopped shelling Landing Zone Bronco from locations inside Duc Pho. Their plan had failed to bring an American assault in which many villagers might be killed, a useful propaganda tool that would have shown how ruthless the Americans could become. The Viet Cong began setting up their mortars outside the village, often at locations in the rice paddies where they had a clearer view of Landing Zone Bronco.

As the nighttime mortar attacks continued, Sergeant Sundvor was growing anxious. "When you're in the field, you have mobility," he told me. "You can move away from danger. But here in base camp, you can't go anywhere except to a bunker, and Charlie knows exactly where you're at."

The nighttime attacks were also heightening my own fears. I was becoming a "short timer," and a strange, uneasy feeling was settling over me. I began doing everything possible to make myself safer.

I avoided traveling in supply convoys down Highway 1. When I had guard duty, I always made certain that Brian Taylor and Chuck Davis were assigned to my bunker. And when I didn't have guard duty, I added one more bandoleer of ammunition at the foot of my cot at night.

One day at dusk, a soldier fired several shots at a poisonous snake outside my tent. I ran out of my tent to see bits of snake flesh on the ground. From that night on, when nightfall approached, I always searched the ground around my tent before going inside. And when I went to bed, I tucked my mosquito net tightly under my bedroll, carefully folding each side to make sure there were no holes.

As my tour moved closer to the end, I didn't dare think of what it might feel like to leave Vietnam. That would be presumptuous and could bring bad luck. Still, I had fleeting thoughts of sitting in a jetliner hurtling down the runway and lifting off from Cam Ranh Bay.

*But first I have to make it to Cam Ranh Bay.*

My only reassurance was that each day, I moved 24 hours closer to leaving Vietnam. But now, my thoughts of survival were more uncertain as the Viet Cong continued their attacks. It seemed as though the Viet Cong were doing everything they could to ruin my departure.

"It's just my fucking luck that Charlie is trying to kick our ass now," I told Sundvor. "I just want to go home."

"Me too!" Sundvor shouted back at me. There was hard sarcasm in his voice.

I nodded and walked out of the supply tent, lighting a cigarette and staring at the mountains. My face was hot and flushed. Suddenly I realized how self-centered I had become. My short-timer's conceit was probably overwhelming for those who knew me, but no one had said anything to me until now. Sundvor only said, "Me too!" But those two words spoke volumes, shaking me out of my smug, self-important stupor.

*Everyone wants to go home. What makes you think you're so fucking special?*

I stubbed my cigarette in the dirt, and looked again to the mountains, wondering where Charlie was at that moment. The only thing that was certain was that he was up there somewhere, planning another attack, probably for that night.

Later, Sundvor and I finished going over the next day's supply requests, and we sat on our cots, talking. "I forgot to mention one thing in our conversation the other night," Sundvor said.

"What?"

"Don't tell anyone what I told you, okay?"

"I won't."

"The other guys who know about it are McDonald and Sanchez, and I know they won't say anything."

"Mum's the word," I said.

Much later that night, the siren sounded. Sundvor and I both swung out of our cots and into our boots, and we were out the door in an instant. We ran to the bunker and rushed inside as a mortar landed nearby. The bunker walls shook, and sand began spilling down from the ceiling.

"Son of a bitch, that was close," Sundvor said.

We found a place to sit along the wall as another

mortar slammed into the ground very close to the bunker. The bunker walls shook again, and sand began pouring down from the ceiling, mixing with the falling dust. The air was suffocating, and someone began coughing. I pulled my shirt up over my mouth and tried to breath.

Another mortar landed nearby, shaking the walls again. The falling dust was growing thicker; now several men were coughing. The falling mortars sounded more distant. "Sounds like Charlie is walking his mortars across camp," someone said.

Dust lingered in the stifling hot air in the bunker. "I can't breathe in this fucking hole," I told Sundvor. "I've got to get some air!"

I got up and ran out the door, leaning against the outside wall and breathing the fresh air. A moment later, Sundvor emerged. We looked toward the helicopter pads as mortars began exploding at opposite ends of the airstrip. The falling mortars began moving toward the center of the airstrip, the explosions illuminating the helicopters. Each time a mortar struck a helicopter, there was a bright flash.

"Son of a bitch, look at that," Sundvor said. "They're walking their fucking mortars down the strip." Several more mortars rained down as they neared the center. There was a yellow flash, and a huge fireball mushroomed up.

"Holy shit, looks like they did a bull's-eye on Colonel Binder's copter," Sundvor said.

It appeared that the Viet Cong were targeting the colonel's helicopter. Maybe they knew about the colonel's early-morning air assaults? Perhaps the colonel had killed some of their Viet Cong compatriots? There was no way of knowing. One thing Charlie didn't know, however, was that the colonel's own men had also been shooting at his helicopter.

A smug grin was forming on my face as we went back inside the bunker, sitting alongside the wall. A half hour passed before a mortar landed nearby, shaking the bunker walls and bringing more dust falling from the ceiling.

The night wore on as we sat huddled inside, trying to breathe in the hot dusty air, listening to the gunfire and explosions outside. We waited impatiently for the morning light, wondering how the firefights were going on the perimeter. I hated sitting inside the bunker. It felt claustrophobic, and you couldn't see what was coming.

As morning broke, the gunfire ended, and the usual surreal calm settled over Landing Zone Bronco. It was a beautiful day, with bright sunshine reflecting off the rice paddies. Farmers seemed to appear out of nowhere and began working in the fields next to the perimeter.

Meanwhile, the brigade support staff began another day of work inside a tent in the far corner of the camp. The tent was the field office of the brigade's Judge Advocate General's (JAG) Corps, the legal branch of the military. The captain who ran the JAG office was a very superstitious man who feared he would not survive Vietnam.

"Get me out of this hellhole as quickly as possible," the captain ordered his legal staff. The mission was clear—find a legal way for the captain to get an early release from Vietnam.

"There's got to be some rule or regulation somewhere," he told his staff. "Now go find it!"

In the weeks that followed, the JAG staff sat in their sweltering-hot tent, poring over documents and books of military regulations and military law. They weren't exactly sure of what they were looking for, but it was a definite change from their typical work involving such things as misconduct by officers or enlisted men.

Then they found the key. Hawaii was considered overseas hardship duty for married soldiers who were stationed in Hawaii but were not given military housing so that their wives could join them. Therefore, when a married soldier's Hawaii overseas duty was added to his Vietnam overseas duty, many married personnel became eligible to rotate early to non-overseas duty. Suddenly dozens of married men in the 11th Brigade were eligible to leave Vietnam early.

During my second week of training Sundvor, I saw Sergeant Padilla approach our supply tent. He walked in the door, holding a piece of paper in his right hand.

'"Good news, Sergeant Sundvor. You're going home."

"What do you mean?" Sundvor asked.

"You're getting an early out. You're going home," Sergeant Padilla repeated. "The army says you've had enough overseas hardship duty since you weren't given military housing for you and your wife when you were stationed in Hawaii."

Sundvor's mouth dropped open, and he stood speechless. First he stared at Padilla, and then he turned and stared at me. Sergeant Padilla grabbed his arm and handed him the paper. "Here, take it," he said.

Suddenly Sundvor let out a shrill scream and jumped high in the air. "Son of a bitch, I'm going home!"

I stepped forward to shake his hand, but he brushed past my outstretched arm and gave me a bear hug.

Just like that, Sundvor's tour ended. He was leaving Vietnam, but I was staying. I tried to appear excited as I grinned at Sundvor, but it was all a lie. My smug short-timer's attitude was stirring again inside me. I was supposed to be the first to leave, and Sundvor was supposed to be my replacement.

Four days later, Sundvor flung his duffel bag into the back of the supply jeep, and I drove him to the airstrip. Landing Zone Bronco looked like a wasteland under the hot morning sun. Several crumpled helicopters remained on the battered airstrip, and there were gaping holes in the ground from the mortars. I drove to the center of the airstrip and slowed so that we could see Colonel Binder's helicopter. Walls of sandbags still stood on three sides of the helicopter, but on the fourth side, the wall was gone, and we could see inside. The colonel's copter was a pile of melted green metal, the rotor blades extending limply from the center of the pile. Two officers were examining the wreckage.

As we drove by, Sundvor grinned. "They beat the shit out of the colonel's helicopter. It looks like it took at least two direct hits," he said.

"That's your going-away present from Charlie," I said.

"Tell Charlie thanks if you see him," Sundvor said, laughing.

Our laughter stopped as we neared the end of the runway, where a large, wide-bodied Chinook helicopter was warming up, its huge rotor blades slowly turning, raising a cloud of dust. The Chinook would fly Sundvor and more than a dozen other soldiers from Duc Pho to Cam Ranh Bay.

I stopped the jeep at the end of the airstrip and jumped out, but Sundvor remained sitting in jeep, staring at the helicopter. Sundvor had a strange look on his face, a look of disbelief. He raised his hands, grasping both sides of his head, and slowly bent forward. Tears were flowing down his cheeks, spilling onto his lap.

I grabbed Sundvor's duffel bag out of the back of the jeep. "It's real," I told him. "You made it. You're going back to the world."

Sundvor remained in the jeep, drying his eyes with his shirt sleeve. I handed him his duffel bag. "Get moving, or you'll miss your flight. Those fucking chopper pilots aren't going to wait on you."

Sundvor looked up and nodded. There were no more

parting words. There was only the helicopter and Sundvor walking toward it. As he climbed the stairs on the side of the helicopter, he paused and waved good-bye through the dust cloud.

I raised my arm high above my head and waved back. Then I got into the jeep and watched the Chinook slowly rise from the ground. The helicopter banked to the left and began flying south toward Cam Ranh Bay. After months of firefights, mortar attacks, exploding mines, and booby traps, Sundvor was leaving.

As I watched the helicopter grow smaller in the distant sky, I knew I would never see Sundvor again. The thought was strangely comforting, not because I disliked Sundvor but because I feared what he might become. There were so many images.

There was Sundvor, the family man, returning home to his wife and kids.

There was Sundvor, the squad leader, admired by his men and his commanding officer.

There was Sundvor, the man who went squirrel hunting with his father but felt sorry for the squirrels.

There was Sundvor, the infantryman who beheaded an old man and dropped the head into the village well.

22 June 1968
Duc Pho


Dear Mom and Dad,

I've got a few minutes before going down to the airstrip to load supplies onto the helicopter, so I'll drop some lines your way.

Sergeant Sundvor, my on-the-job replacement, went back to the world because his wife wasn't command sponsored while we were stationed in Hawaii. In other words, the army didn't provide them military housing in Hawaii, so that's considered overseas hardship duty. So now I have to start training a new guy all over again. I was glad to see Sundvor get out of Vietnam early, but it didn't help me much here.

We had some bad luck two days ago. Our former commander, Captain Lewis, was killed when his helicopter was shot down. I worked for him for more than a year. He was always good to me—gave me lots of breaks. Anyway, he's gone now, so there's nothing else I can say that will change anything. The battalion commanding officer was also on the helicopter, and he was also killed, along with the helicopter crew.

*Our company moved north last week and then west. Now they're only 13 miles from Laos. My supply lines keep getting stretched farther out, and now it's a 40-minute helicopter ride to their field position. It's NVA territory up there, a bad area for American infantry to patrol.*

*Your son,*
*Alan*

# Chapter 12

# War Without End

As the searing Vietnamese summer dragged on, more B Company men fell in combat. By midsummer, almost all of the original infantrymen were gone, either dead or wounded or, like Sergeant Sundvor, they rotated out early from Vietnam.

I continued my frequent trips to a newly established "replacement center," a large tent near the airstrip, to pick up those who were assigned to B Company. I didn't say "welcome" to any of the men; instead, I silently assigned them their weapons and gear and told them when we would be going to the field.

Harris and I still had our graves registration duties. I remember one particularly muggy, hot day when Harris was in a very bad mood. He cursed as he searched through his files in his tent, looking for a dead soldier's dental records.

The dental records, along with the soldier's other medical records, would be sent with the body to the United States. When Harris couldn't find the dental chart, he called division headquarters.

"Don't worry about that," they said. "He doesn't have a head."

Many of B Company's casualties were like that— bodies mutilated by war. Harris identified them all. And perhaps most depressing to Harris and me was the certainty that this deadly process would continue. It seemed as though the war was going from bad to worse.

Still, the replacements continued to arrive. They often were fresh out of boot camp and wearing clean fatigues. Their faces were shaved, and they casually joked with one another. As I issued them their weapons and gear, some said they were looking forward to this new Vietnam adventure.

"I want to kick some ass over here," a replacement told me one day as I handed him his M16.

"You're wrong," I told him. "You need to keep your head down and your ass close to the ground, or Charlie will blow you away. And watch for booby traps; they've got them planted everywhere."

A few days later, my hard demeanor softened a bit when a replacement named Private Rob Anteal arrived at my tent. He had a quiet manner and stood tall with short blond hair.

"Been here long, Sergeant?" he asked as I handed him his gear.

"Going on seven months," I said. "I'm getting short. Only a couple of months to go."

"Me too," Private Anteal said. "I've only got 12 months left."

We both laughed. It felt good to laugh.

"I worked as a supply clerk for two months after finishing boot camp at Fort Benning, Georgia," Anteal said. "Then one day, I got my orders to come to Vietnam. I would have preferred staying stateside and working in supply. How about you?"

"After boot camp at Fort Dix, New Jersey, they sent me to Hawaii," I said. "Damn, I would have liked to stay in Hawaii, but our brigade was doing combat jungle training there, so the writing was on the wall."

"Married?" Private Anteal asked.

"Nope," I said. "How about you?"

"I got hitched right out of college," he answered. "When I get out of the army and go home, I expect to find my wife just like I left her."

"How's that?" I asked.

"Freshly fucked," he replied.

We laughed again, and I gave him the rest of his gear. The next day, Captain Hershell called me on the radio. "Has Private Anteal arrived?" he asked.

"Yes sir, he got here yesterday," I said.

"I saw on his orders that he worked in supply for some time after basic training," the captain said. "So I want you to give him a crash course in the duties of supply sergeant so that he can take over when you leave."

"Yes sir," I answered. "How long should I train him?"

"I'll give you two weeks," Captain Hershell said. "Then send him out to the field. We're too short of men out here to keep him in base camp. Then, when you're nearing the end of your tour, I'll send Private Anteal back to base camp so that he can get ready to replace you."

"Yes sir," I answered.

I walked down the path leading to the replacement tent, went inside, and found Private Anteal lying on a cot, reading a paperback book. "This is a good book," he said as I approached.

"What is it?" I asked.

"*Travels with Charlie* by John Steinbeck," he answered. "He and his dog are on a road trip, going all over the United States."

"Where are they now?" I asked.

"They're traveling through North Dakota," Anteal said. "I've never been there. Have you?

"That's where I'm from," I said.

Anteal looked surprised. "You're the first guy I've met from North Dakota."

"I hear that all the time," I said. "There aren't many of us."

Anteal laughed. "I'm from Indiana, but I guess it doesn't matter much where we're from as long as we're stationed in this piss hole."

"That's the first time I've ever heard anyone refer to Vietnam as a piss hole," I said. "I could probably think of even worse names for this place."

We laughed, and I sat down on an empty cot facing Anteal. "I've got good news for you. Captain Hershell wants me to train you so that you can take over supply when I leave."

Anteal's face seemed to light up. "For real?" he asked.

"That's affirmative," I said. "The last man I started to train got an early out, so there's no one to replace me. The army can't find enough replacements for casualties in the field, so it's unlikely they'll find a supply sergeant."

Private Anteal got up from his cot and reached out to shake my hand. I didn't expect this, and I responded in an awkward manner, limply returning the handshake. Anteal seemed to know how important this news was for him, and I sensed he was waiting for me to say more.

"I'm not going to mince words," I said. "Your chances of surviving this war are one hell of a lot better here in base camp than out in the field. We've had lots of casualties in the field. But here in base camp, it's much safer. You usually don't go on patrol, and you have guard duty only once every third night. You'll be flying a lot on the supply helicopter, and sometimes that can get dicey when Charlie starts shooting at you, but it's still better than being on the ground."

Anteal listened intently to everything I said, nodding

his head as I spoke.

"The old man wants me to train you for two weeks and then send you to the field for a while. Then, when I'm down to my final month, you'll come back to base camp to replace me."

"Yes sir," Anteal responded. "When do I start training?"

"Come to my tent at 0600 hours tomorrow," I said.

I felt good as I began walking back to my supply tent. Although I had known Private Anteal for only a short while, I enjoyed his quiet manner and his sense of humor. I knew he would become a good supply sergeant for B Company. Even more importantly, I knew his chances of surviving the Vietnam War were far better now. With a little bit of luck, Private Anteal would one day return home to his wife in Indiana.

The next morning, Anteal moved his gear to the supply tent. I showed him the empty cot where Sundvor had slept. Anteal laid his things on the cot, and I started training him. As with Sergeant Sundvor, Anteal was a good student, taking the supply requests over the radio and assembling them in our tent for transport to the helicopter pad.

Two weeks later, we boarded the supply helicopter and flew out to the field. After unloading the supplies, Anteal turned to say good-bye.

"I'll see you soon in base camp," I said. "In the meantime, keep your ass low to the ground, and don't step on any mines or booby traps. I don't want to have to train another man for supply."

Anteal laughed and walked away.

In the days that followed, when the resupply helicopter arrived in the field, Anteal was usually waiting to help me unload the supplies. We joked with one another, and he told me how anxious he was to return to base camp.

Then one day, I noticed a subtle change in his manner. For the first time, his face was somber, and his sense of humor, gone. "There's some bad shit going on out here," he said.

"What's going on?" I asked.

"You know," he said. "Bad shit." He described, in graphic detail, the mutilated bodies of friends who were killed or wounded. And he told me how much he hated the villagers, with their hard, defiant looks as the company searched their huts.

The war was changing Private Anteal. The calm look on his face was gone. He had been in the field only a few weeks, but he already looked like a hardened infantryman, a 23-year-old with a gun and a license to kill.

The unthinkable happened one day as B Company entered a small, nearly deserted village. The company commander believed the village was mostly used as a base for Viet Cong and ordered the village burned to the ground.

Squads of GIs fanned out and began systematically searching the thatched huts to remove the few people who were still there. When Anteal entered a hut, he saw an old man cowering on the floor.

Anteal shouted at him, "Di di mau," but the elderly man remained on the floor. "Di di mau," Anteal repeated in a louder voice, but the old man wasn't moving; he didn't want to leave his home.

Anteal's face hardened and he clenched his teeth as he dragged the old man to the center of the hut, tying him to the pole that supported the roof. Then he piled baskets, clothing and other material at the old man's feet. Anteal had reached the breaking point. He was spiraling into a dark abyss filled with hate, confusion and rage. He was eager to kill. He set fire to the baskets at the old man's feet, and rushed out of the hut. Then he set fire to the outside wall. Other infantrymen were still sweeping through the village, ushering the remaining villagers out of their huts and setting fires. Anteal lingered outside the old man's hut, listening to the man scream as he burned to death.

One week after committing the atrocity, Anteal returned to base camp and told me what he had done. Unlike Sundvor's confession, there was no remorse, no tears—only hatred. In the days that followed, I was surprised when I heard Anteal brag to other soldiers what he had done. Private Anteal was now a bona fide killer. Even worse, he was proud of it. He might even brag about it to his friends when he returned home to Indiana.

But Anteal would never return home. Two weeks after he arrived in base camp, he was driving the supply jeep on Highway 1 near Duc Pho. As he approached a grove of palm trees, he was ambushed by Viet Cong. Anteal was shot in the neck, and the jeep swerved off the road. An infantry patrol soon found Anteal unconscious, slumped over the steering wheel but still breathing. They called for a medical-evacuation helicopter, but Anteal died before it arrived.

5 July 1968
Duc Pho

Dear Claire and Edwin,

I'm sorry I haven't written you for a long time, but I've been busy as hell ever since I returned from R&R in Australia. I've got perimeter guard tonight, so it gives me some time to write a letter (it isn't dark here yet).

I had a great time on my R&R in Australia. Lots of friendly women (or "birds," as they say down there) and swinging clubs, and the weather was perfect. It was fall season Down Under and a welcome relief from the constant heat in Vietnam.

It was really a letdown coming back here, but after you've been back a week or so, you forget there really is a world out there where nobody is shooting at each other. I don't want to sound too sarcastic, but I'm getting short, so I can't help it.

Well, it's getting dark, so I'll sign off. I sent you a Mother's Day gift from Australia, Claire, but after I sent it I found out it will take six weeks to get to you. They sent it by boat and didn't tell me that until after I purchased it.

PS: I'm writing this the following evening. Last night, after I wrote the letter to you, we had another attack. Charlie threw in 140 mortars and rockets on our base camp. We took a direct hit on our field-hospital tent, which has a large red cross painted on top. But Charlie doesn't care if he kills people in a hospital, because he's a dirty bastard.

Many tents and bunkers were destroyed, and several of our helicopters took direct hits. Charlie keeps smashing the hell out of the copters on the airstrip, I guess so we can't fly out. All total, there were 44 casualties for the base. We expect another attack tonight, so everyone is getting ready.

Alan

# Chapter 13

## Searching for a Snake in the Brush

The killing of Private Anteal ended any future plans for training someone to replace myself as supply sergeant. "We just don't have enough men in the field," the company commander told me. "So when you rotate out, I'll just send someone into camp to replace you, and you should ask the C Company supply sergeant to train your replacement."

"Yes sir," I said. "I'll talk to the C Company sergeant to give him a heads-up."

Meanwhile, Harris' ETS was fast approaching, and I dreaded the day that he would leave. Then, Harris received his orders. I heard him shouting for joy in his nearby tent. Moments later, he burst into the supply tent, holding the paper. I stood and shook his hand. "Son of a bitch, I'm going to miss you," I said. "It's not going to be the same around here."

"Well, you're not too far behind me," Harris said. "You'll be catching that big bird and going home soon."

Two days later, I drove Harris to the airstrip. All of the

battered helicopters had been removed, but the base camp still looked like a wasteland with several craters lining the runway. The nearby drab green army tents seemed to sag under the boiling sun. I drove Harris to the end of the airstrip, where the Chinook helicopter was warming up, its rotor blades slowly swinging to life.

"Keep your head down, and don't step on any booby-trapped grenades," Harris said, grinning. "You'll be home soon." He got out of the jeep and began walking briskly toward the Chinook.

I waved good-bye as Harris reached the helicopter and bound up the stairway. The Chinook's blades were gaining speed, raising the cloud of dust.

I sat in my jeep, watching the giant Chinook tilt forward and lift up from the ground. The Chinook banked to the left as it flew away. I lingered there, watching it, and after a few minutes, it was just a small black object far off in the sky. An empty feeling swept over me. It seemed as though everyone was leaving Vietnam—everyone except me.

I started the jeep and began driving back toward my supply tent, thinking of all the things that Harris and I shared in the war. We constantly worked to put back what was taken from B Company, but it was a futile task, and we both knew it. We simply did our jobs, as assigned by the army, and we collaborated on many levels. We operated as a close-knit, two-person team, conducting a smooth, seamless operation with almost no disagreements. I couldn't think of anyone whom I would rather have worked with.

Two days later, shortly before sundown, a medic rushed into my tent. "Lieutenant Chang wants you up in the medic tent right away," he said. "And bring your M16."

"What the fuck for?" I asked.

"Just come along with me," the medic said, sounding annoyed.

I grabbed my M16 and followed him. When we entered the medic's tent, I saw Private Jim Guthrie lying on a cot. He was naked from the waist down, his right leg covered in blood and swollen. "Give me something!" he screamed at Lieutenant Chang. Then he began shaking his head back and forth, moaning in pain.

Lieutenant Chang grabbed the soldier's shoulders and stared at his face as if to steady him on the cot. "We've got to go find it first, and then I'll know which antivenom to give you."

The lieutenant turned and faced me. "Sergeant Quale, I need you to come with me to find the snake." He stepped forward and handed me a flashlight. The medic went to the cot to watch over the injured man as Lieutenant Chang and I left the tent. As we followed a trail down the hill, the lieutenant described what happened.

"Private Guthrie was walking on this trail to the shower tent." The lieutenant stopped and turned on his flashlight, shining it in front of us to where the trail entered the bushes. "He was walking there, through the bushes, when he felt something scrape his ankle. He thought it was a sharp branch so he kicked it to clear it from the trail. But it wasn't a branch; it was a snake. The snake bit him at least seven times. He panicked, running up to our tent screaming."

The lieutenant shook his head. "And Guthrie didn't kill the snake, so now we need to find it so that I'll know which antivenom to give him. When we find the snake, I want you to shoot it."

I nodded, and we moved into the brush. The daylight was fading as we began pulling back branches to look underneath, swinging our flashlights back and forth, moving cautiously forward.

My stomach was turning into a tight knot, a familiar feeling in Vietnam, but this time it was different. There were no falling mortars, no Viet Cong advancing on my bunker. This time there was a deadly snake in the brush, and if we didn't soon find it, a young man's life might be in jeopardy.

We moved slowly through the dense vegetation, our flashlights casting ghoulish images on the ground as the light shined through the branches. I could almost taste my fear, knowing the snake was likely still there, hiding somewhere. We moved halfway through the bushes, searching in silence.

"Maybe there's more than one?" I asked in a loud voice, anxious to break the quiet.

"It's possible," Lieutenant Chang said.

My stomach grew tighter. We continued moving, pulling shrubs to the side, shining our flashlights underneath and lowering our heads to see if the snake was there.

"Here's something," Lieutenant Chang suddenly shouted. I rushed to where he stood, pulling branches up on a bush. We both shined our lights underneath, where a large, twisted branch lay on the ground. "Nope, that's not it," the lieutenant said.

I was growing frustrated. "Where the hell is it?" I asked.

The lieutenant didn't respond, he continued moving through the brush. I looked up at the sky; it was growing darker, and our search was starting to feel hopeless. The approaching night would soon shroud everything in darkness, providing cover once again for something dangerous.

Still, Lieutenant Chang pressed on, and I followed. We searched for almost an hour, moving through the brush, scanning the ground under the bushes with our flashlights.

Finally, the lieutenant stepped out of the vegetation onto the trail and turned toward me. "Shit, we're never going to find it. It's too dark."

We walked single file back toward the medic's tent, our flashlights still scanning the ground. We could hear Guthrie moaning as we approached.

When we entered the tent, Guthrie turned to look at us. His face was twisted with pain, and his eyes grew wide as we approached. Lieutenant Chang stopped a couple of feet from the cot. "We couldn't find the snake," he said.

Guthrie's mouth dropped open, and an anguished look spread across his face. "Am I going to die?" he asked.

"Of course not," Chang said as he went to a nearby cabinet. "I'll give you a shot of the antivenom that's used here." The lieutenant glanced at his medic and shrugged, looking uncertain. I watched as the lieutenant slid the needle into Guthrie's arm, simultaneously trying to comfort him. "You're going to be all right; the antivenom will start working soon."

Still, there was a worried look on the lieutenant's face as he looked at Guthrie's leg. While injecting the antivenom he placed his other hand on the leg to examine the swelling. "No, don't touch it!" Guthrie screamed. "That hurts!"

The lieutenant finished injecting the antivenom and stepped back, exchanging nervous glances with his medic. Guthrie cried out again in pain, and then his shoulders slumped flat on the cot. He began moaning, simultaneously shaking his head back and forth. "Ohhhhhh, fuck, my leg hurts!"

"I'll also give you something for the pain," the lieutenant said as he walked back to the cabinet.

The moment seemed right, so I laid my flashlight on a

table. "Well, sir, I guess you're done with my services?" I was anxious to get out of the tent and away from Guthrie as he moaned and shook in pain. His leg was swollen so large that you could easily see the holes in the flesh where the snake bit him.

"Yes, you're done here," the lieutenant said. "I'll know who to call if there's another snake in the brush." A grin was forming on the lieutenant's face.

"I'm not that good at finding snakes," I said, grinning back at the lieutenant. "You don't have to call me."

Our brief moment of levity ended as I stepped out of the tent. I was worried about Guthrie. We didn't find the snake that bit him and now we could only hope that the antivenom given by Lieutenant Chang would work. As I walked toward my tent the night was growing darker, and I stumbled on a rock, almost dropping my M16.

"Son of a bitch!" I screamed. I reached down and found the rock, picking it up and flinging it hard to the side.

My face was growing tight with frustration and anger. Suddenly I realized how much I despised everything around me — the drab green army tents, the suffocating bunkers on the perimeter and the snake still hiding somewhere in the brush. I hated the Viet Cong who, at that moment, were likely descending the nearby mountains, preparing to attack us.

Everything was hopeless. There would be no end to the misery, pain and death. No one was safe, including a young man who went to shower and now lay crying in pain, his log grossly swollen, punctured with snake bites.

I wiped the sweat off my forehead with the back of my hand, trying to calm my anger. Then I took a deep breath, but the air was stifling and smelled of decaying foliage.

I wanted to curse out loud, but I clinched my teeth and went inside my tent. I found my flashlight and stepped outside, conducting my nightly ritual, searching the ground around my tent, which seemed to calm my anger. Before going back inside, I shined my flashlight down the hill to where the trail entered the bushes near the shower tent. I had walked on that trail many times at sunset, wearing only sandals with a towel wrapped around my waist, just like Guthrie, anxious to take a cool shower at the end of a hot day.

*Was the snake in the bushes when I passed by?*

I couldn't be sure, but I knew one thing for certain. I would never again walk on that trail through the brush at sundown. I was imposing one more rule to follow in Vietnam, one more thing to help me make it to the end.

*17 July 1968*
*Duc Pho*

*Dear Mom and Dad,*

*I just finished eating dinner (fish again), and I've got a few minutes before going back to work, so I'll write a few lines. I can hardly concentrate on my work anymore. All I can say is it's a good thing I'm getting short.*

*Last week, another guy and I drove a one-jeep convoy to Chu Lai, which is about 50 miles from here. We picked up beer and soda in Chu Lai, filling the jeep's trailer, and returned to Duc Pho. The company doesn't like it when I run out of refreshments to send to them. I guess it was a pretty foolish thing to do, driving by ourselves on Highway 1 and not in a convoy with other vehicles. But they say Highway 1 is more secure these days.*

*Still, every time I drive down Highway 1, things look worse than they did before. More bridges and more railway tracks are blown up, and generally there is more destruction everywhere. Things here in Vietnam just don't get any better; they seem worse every day.*

*Nothing much has happened here in Duc Pho lately, although they had a small mortar-and-rocket attack when I was in Chu Lai. I guess I picked a good time to leave.*

*Well, I've got about 19 days until I leave Vietnam. Looking* back, I didn't think I'd ever get this short, but here it is—just 19 days and a plane crash. (Ha)

A guy was bitten seven times by a snake last week near the medic's tent. The medics gave him antivenom, but his leg still swelled up so much that they had to lance his leg in several places during the night. They evacuated him to Qui Nhon the next morning. The last I heard, he's going to live, although I'm sure his leg will be sore as hell for a long time. It was pretty much his fault that he was bitten, because he was going through the bushes wearing only thongs, and he wasn't watching where he walked; that's a big mistake in a place like Vietnam.

More of the guys that I work with in B Company's headquarters section are leaving here for civilian life. Harris, the company clerk, left last week, and then our company armorer left yesterday. The original members of B Company are almost all gone. I don't know a hell of a lot of the men in B Company anymore.

Alan

*18 July 1968*
*Duc Pho*
*(Nice place if you're a VC)*

Dear Claire and Edwin,

It's 10 a.m., and although I should be working, I'll cheat Uncle Sam and write you a few lines. I guess I'm getting a bad case of short timer's attitude.

I've been trying to stay safe here. I had volunteered to be a courier on a flight to a landing zone north of Da Nang, but I changed my mind and sent someone else in my place. (I'm too short to travel.)

As far as my civilian plans go, I don't know what I'm going to do when I get out. I'm sure I'll find something to do other than wear green clothes and carry a gun.

I was thinking perhaps I might like to teach, although I'd have to go back to college and get a certificate. I might enjoy teaching social science. Hmmm, I get so excited talking about civilian life that I can almost taste it.

When I look back at my two years in the army, it seems like a long time, especially the nine months over here. Vietnam has been an experience, although I'm not sure if it was a good experience. At any rate, I'm going to readjust to civilian life and forget about this mess.

I don't have long until I'm forced to leave the exotic orient, but you might have enough time to send me one *more letter if you want; however, you probably should discontinue sending copies of the hometown newspaper, since it takes longer to get here. I really appreciate you sending the newspapers; they were my touch with the world.*

*Thanks,*
*Alan*

*26 July 1968*
*Duc Pho*

*Dear Carol and Wally,*

*The water has turned stale here with the summer heat, and I've contracted a bad case of "jungle rot." Your skin just kind of dies and flakes off. Just about everyone has it. When I saw the battalion doctor about my jungle rot, I learned he also went to the University of North Dakota. So we got to talking about the good old days back in college, and he never did say what to do about the rot. I guess I'll just have to ETS and go back to the world where hygiene exists.*

*The dirty bastards assigned me to be the sergeant of the guard tonight (they won't even let us short timers off). I'll be responsible for 12 bunkers, which covers a good portion of the perimeter, so it can get a little hairy. Plus, I'm responsible for the guards inside the perimeter. We've got guards everywhere these days.*

*I'm down to just a few days and a plane crash before I leave this hellhole. Our battalion is now patrolling pretty much along the Laos border. That's North Vietnamese army territory up there, and it's very mountainous. They haven't moved me up there yet. Needless to say, I could do without seeing that part of Vietnam. I've got my fingers crossed that they won't move me up there prior to my ETS.*

*I guess I better stop complaining about everything over here. I know I've become bitter about this war, and I'll probably stay bitter until everyone gets out of this God-forsaken place. It will be nice when I finally leave Vietnam, but I will never feel right until they stop sending Americans to this place. Every time I see another replacement walk into my tent, I feel like shit.*

*What a waste.*

*Alan*

# Chapter 14

# Welcome Home

Four weeks after Private Anteal was killed, I received my orders to leave Vietnam. Corporal Brad Davis, the new company clerk, handed me the papers.

"You're lucky your leaving," he said. Davis was 20 years old, and drafted into the military shortly after finishing junior college. "I wish it was me who was leaving," he said. "I hate this war."

"Sorry, but you're shit out of luck," I said, grinning at him. "It's my turn to go." I stared at the stack of papers on his desk. "What's all that?" I asked.

"I'm compiling the monthly Company B report for brigade headquarters," he said. "As you know, there were two killed this month, Anteal and Brown, and 14 others wounded, which brings the total to 19 killed and 83 wounded since B Company arrived in Vietnam."

Davis got up from his desk and lit a cigarette, blowing the smoke toward the doorway. "I hate doing this list," he said. "It's so fucking impersonal, there are only numbers, no names."

The following morning I said goodbye to Davis and

we shook hands. "You'll be heading home soon to Detroit," I told him. "Say hello to Diana Ross and the Supremes when you get there." He laughed and I left his tent, walking across the pathway and into my supply tent.

My replacement was Corporal Andrew Wyatt, age 25, whose thick brown hair stuck out the sides of his helmet. He was sent from the field to base camp five days earlier to replace me. I handed Wyatt my M16 rifle and showed him where he could log the transaction in the supply records. I watched as the corporal briefly examined my rifle before locking it in the gun rack. The other rifles in the rack were new; I had unpacked them from their crates days earlier. The new weapons looked clean and shiny next to my used M16, which was covered with scratches, its black stock faded from exposure to the Vietnam sun.

As I stared at my M16, I felt like I was leaving part of me behind. The rifle had always been with me, hanging from my shoulder, facing out the bunker window or lying on the floor next to my cot at night.

I walked out of the supply tent, tossed my duffel bag into the jeep, and Corporal Wyatt drove me to the airstrip. The big Chinook helicopter was warming up, its giant rotor blades slowly swinging to life, raising the usual cloud of dust. I grabbed my duffel bag and jumped out of the jeep, thanking the corporal for the ride. After walking briskly to the Chinook, I turned to wave good-bye, but the jeep was already gone. I laughed out loud. *Why should Wyatt wait to wave good-bye? We don't even know each other.*

The Chinook slowly lifted up and banked to the right,

climbing higher as we passed over Duc Pho. The village looked small and crowded from the air. The ARVN bunker stood out in the middle of town, its high walls reflecting the morning sun. I tried to locate the orphanage to see if the boys were gathered at the gate, but the helicopter banked to the left, and Duc Pho disappeared from view.

After arriving in Cam Ranh Bay, I was quickly processed and given my boarding pass on a jetliner. The next morning, it was hot and sunny as we boarded the plane. I recognized several other soldiers from Landing Zone Bronco. Once we were all on board, the pilots started the engines, and soon the aircraft rumbled down the runway. The plane lifted off, passing over a white-sand beach and above the blue ocean. I turned in my seat for one last glimpse of the tall, emerald mountains rising up near the beach. Puffy white clouds rested above the peaks. It was a beautiful sight, this last glimpse of Vietnam. But no one on the plane cared about the scenery, and when the jetliner's wheels left the runaway, the cabin was filled with loud cheers. I continued staring out my window, watching Vietnam fade into the distance as the jetliner headed out to sea.

Soon the cabin grew quiet, and several men began settling into their seats to sleep, while others flipped through magazines. There would be no alcoholic drinks served on this long flight, and the stewardesses quickly disappeared into the front galley shortly after takeoff. When they did reappear, delivering coffee, snacks, and soft drinks, they looked uncomfortable, almost frightened.

None of the stewardesses smiled at any soldiers on the plane, not once.

I looked around, examining my fellow passengers. We were a motley crew, with our torn, stained jungle fatigues. Many men were unshaved with disheveled hair. The air in the cabin was already growing stale with body odor.

*No wonder the stewardesses aren't smiling at us.*

As the jetliner flew eastward, the hours passed, and the sky slowly turned dark. The tedium of sitting on a jetliner made me drowsy. I slept on and off through most of the long flight, awakening occasionally to look out the window. But there was only darkness. Much later, I was awakened by the voice of the captain on the intercom. The night was gone and the bright sun was shining through the windows.

"We're about to begin our descent to Fort Lewis," the captain said. "When the light comes on, please fasten your seat belt."

The jetliner descended slowly from sunshine into the dark clouds covering the Pacific Northwest. The cabin grew quiet as we stared out the windows at the grayness and beads of rain streaking across the glass. The plane slowly swung to one side and then leveled off and continued its descent. All eyes were fixed on the windows, waiting to see our first glimpse of America.

The jetliner dropped below the cloud layer, and we saw forest and scattered fields. We passed over a farm with a large, red barn. With the heavy cloud cover, the land looked faded green, the same color as our jungle fatigues.

The plane dropped lower, passing over a stream and forest. The forest abruptly ended, and the jetliner descended over rows of lights, landing on the runway. Cheers filled the cabin, and several troops shook hands and patted each other on the back. We were finally home.

The army had streamlined its outprocessing center for Vietnam veterans. After landing, we were herded onto buses and driven across Fort Lewis to an area where there were long rows of buildings that looked like warehouses.

Each building was used for a single function, and the sign at our first stop said "Station 1 – Footwear". When we entered the building, we were told to remove our jungle boots and toss them into a nearby pile. Then our feet were measured, and we were given new dress shoes.

Station 2 was for uniforms. I removed my fatigues, tossing them onto the pile of fatigues. Then we were told to move to the next station, where we would be fitted with new uniforms. I looked back at the mound of jungle fatigues. I could see my name tag and the sergeant stripes on the sleeves. A strange feeling swept over me. I didn't want to leave my fatigues lying there on the floor; it just didn't seem right. I wanted to take them home.

An army sergeant who was escorting our group saw me staring at the pile and announced, "Gentlemen, you're not allowed to take any of your Vietnam clothing with you."

By the end of the morning, we were all fitted with new uniforms with our ranks sewn on the shoulders and Vietnam service ribbons, insignia, and medals pinned on the front. There were several large mirrors at the side of the room, where we could view ourselves.

I stared at my sudden transformation in the mirror. My uniform was perfectly fitted and neatly pressed, and the polished brass buttons shined bright. But it didn't look right. It looked superficial. It looked like the army was stripping me of any evidence of where I had been.

We continued moving to more stations until all of our paperwork was complete. Then we boarded buses, which took us to a large parking lot near the entrance to the base. The bus driver pulled up to the curb and announced, "Gentlemen, this is where you will sign out of military service."

We began filing out of the bus and walking toward a row of nearby tables, where army clerks motioned for us to step forward. When I reached the front of the line, I gave the clerk a copy of my ETS sheet. The clerk filed the sheet in a box below the table and asked me to print and sign my name, military serial number, and unit. Once I signed my name, he said, "There are civilian buses and taxis over there." He pointed to the side of the parking lot.

I joined a group of men I recognized from Landing Zone Bronco, and the four of us climbed into a taxi. I sat in the front, and the three others sat in the back.

"We're going to Seattle airport," I told the driver.

"You mean SeaTac," he said.

"I guess so."

"Just get us out of this fucking military base," someone in the backseat mumbled.

The cab passed through the base gate and headed down a busy thoroughfare toward Interstate 5. As the cab driver pulled onto the freeway, he accelerated to merge into traffic. I turned and looked at the men in the back; everyone had a big smile on his face. We all stared at the busy freeway traffic, a strange sight after months in Vietnam.

A car filled with young men pulled up alongside our cab, and two of them turned to look at us as though they were inspecting our new army uniforms. Then they both gave us the finger.

"What the fuck?" someone shouted in the backseat. "Did you see that?"

"Why are they giving us the finger?" I asked the cab driver.

The driver, flustered and embarrassed, struggled to find the right words. "Some of people around here, uh…some of them don't like the military very much."

"Well, fuck them," someone shouted in the backseat. There was a sudden rush of air as all the windows rolled down. Everyone's arms were out the windows, returning the gesture to the men in the other car. One of the soldiers in the back of the cab leaned his head and shoulders out the window. "Fuck you!" he screamed.

"Hey," the cab driver said. "Hey! You've got to stay inside the cab!"

The flustered cab driver deliberately slowed down, and the other car sped away, disappearing into the traffic in front of us.

The guys in the backseat rolled up the windows, and the cab grew quiet as the driver slowly increased the speed of the taxi. The excitement over coming home was suddenly gone—at least for the moment—ruined by men in a passing car.

As I looked at the traffic, I wondered what other reactions there might be. We knew the Vietnam War was increasingly unpopular in the United States, but we never thought the Americans would blame us for *their* war. If anyone should be blamed for the war, it should be the politicians in Washington and the people who sent us to Vietnam. But now I feared we were proved wrong on a busy freeway in Tacoma, Washington, only minutes after signing out of the army. There was no mistake over what happened. When the young men flipped their middle fingers at us, it wasn't a frivolous gesture; the looks on their faces were hard and scornful. They meant it.

As I stared at the traffic, I had one other unsettling thought. The last time anyone had given me the finger was months earlier in Duc Pho, when the village boys mobbed our jeep near the orphanage. But somehow, the actions of the boys in Duc Pho seemed less surprising. After all, we were foreign troops in their country.

*But now we're home and Americans are giving us the finger and we're giving them the finger back. What the fuck is up with that?*

\*\*\*

In the weeks that followed, I quickly learned it was not going to be easy being a Vietnam veteran in America, especially in the late 1960s at the height of the antiwar movement. Often, there were hard, unsmiling looks when people learned I had recently returned from Vietnam. Their rigid stares were followed with the usual questions and comments:

"Were there lots of drug addicts in the army?"

"Did soldiers really try to kill their officers?"

"Why did you lose so many men?"

"You guys didn't know how to fight."

"You lost the war."

On more than one occasion, I heard people refer to Vietnam veterans as "baby killers."

Many times, when I was asked about my experiences in Vietnam, I could see the look of disbelief forming on the questioner's face as soon as I started to respond. It seemed that many Americans had no faith in Vietnam veterans. *After all, what did we know? We were drug addicts, heartless killers, and men who didn't know how to fight.*

I tried not to dwell on the disturbing reactions. It was

time for me to return to civilian life, time to find a job. I gathered some personal papers, including a copy of my journalism degree, at my parents' home in Montana, where they had moved after I graduated from college. I drove south to Denver and submitted my first job application at a metropolitan newspaper. After filling out several forms, I was asked to return that afternoon for an interview. When I later returned, I was ushered into an office, where I met a middle-age man wearing a crumpled suit. He was standing behind his desk and reached out to shake my hand.

"I just started reading your application a few minutes ago, and I see you just got out of the army in Vietnam," he began. "What did you do over there?"

"I was a supply sergeant for an infantry company." He nodded, and we both sat down.

"I'm sorry I haven't read the rest of your application, so some of my questions might seem repetitive," he said.

"That's okay."

"What did you do before the army?" he asked.

"I graduated from the University of North Dakota with a degree in journalism."

He glanced at my resume, and then looked up. "Any experience working on a daily newspaper?"

"I worked part-time at the Grand Forks Herald when I was in college, but that was it," I said. "I didn't have a chance to get a regular newspaper job because I received my draft notice the same day I graduated."

He smiled and looked at my application again. "Any references?" he asked.

I reached in my pocket and pulled out a sheet of paper titled "Letter of Appreciation" from J. T. Greenberg, the chief property officer whom I worked with at Landing Zone Bronco. " I have this from the army," I said, handing the paper to him.

He seemed a little puzzled as he looked at the paper. After a moment, he started reading it out loud:

"To Sergeant Alan Quale, I certainly would be remiss in my duties if I failed to commend you for the superlative manner in which you carried out the duties of supply sergeant. The way you have approached the myriad of details surrounding the resupply of an infantry company under combat conditions is just another reason that I want to commend you for a job well done.

"Your interest, initiative, and willingness to learn have enabled you to master the complex problems encountered in the deployment of an infantry company."

The newspaperman paused for a moment, still staring at the letter. I wasn't sure if he was making fun of me. My face was hot with embarrassment. It was a mistake handing him the reference. He cleared his throat and started reading again.

"The many improvements in supply procedures during the previous year have been the result of your diligence and high sense of responsibility.

J. T. Greenberg."

The newspaperman looked up and handed the letter back to me. There was an awkward moment as we stared across his desk at one another.

"It's the only reference I have," I said, shrugging my shoulders. "I know it doesn't have anything to do with journalism, but I thought it might help."

He nodded his head. "Well, we don't have any openings now. Plus, you need to get some experience on a daily newspaper. I suggest you drive up to Wyoming and see if there's an opening at one of the smaller dailies in Laramie—or maybe Casper. Then you can come back and see us in a year or two, and there might be an opening."

We stood and shook hands, and he ushered me to the office door. "Good luck, Sergeant."

I found my way out of the newspaper building and paused on the sidewalk, looking up at the tall buildings of downtown Denver. Heavy traffic filled the street, and a siren was sounding from somewhere nearby. *Maybe he's right,* I thought. *Maybe I have to start at some smaller place. I don't have any experience other than war, and that doesn't count for anything.*

I spent a restless night in my motel room in Denver. After breakfast the next morning, I decided to follow the newspaperman's advice and started driving north. The cities in Wyoming are few and far in between, but in the days that followed, I stopped at a half dozen towns, applying for work at their newspapers. There were no newspaper jobs for me in Wyoming, so I continued driving north into Montana.

Two days after arriving in Montana, I was offered a reporting job at a newspaper in Great Falls. I didn't know what to expect when I arrived for work, but the newsroom staff, which was predominately young, welcomed me to the job. No one asked me about Vietnam, and I seldom talked about it.

My first news story was about a pack of wild dogs killing sheep in a rural area nearby. This was big news in Montana, and my story appeared on the front page. The following day, as I drove to work, I heard my story broadcast on the local radio news. My ego soared, and I felt really good walking into the newsroom that morning.

I quickly fell in love with my newspaper reporter job. It was interesting work, interviewing all sorts of people, covering a wide variety of stories, and occasionally seeing my byline above a story on the front page. Every day was different, depending on the news. I had left the tedium of Vietnam behind, and I was moving forward in my new civilian life. My life was beginning to feel very good.

Winter was fast approaching, and as frigid winds swept down over the northern plains, Vietnam seemed like a distant place. Still, there were times when the memories returned. Sometimes while driving my car, I pulled to the side of the road and looked out the window at the ice and snow, wondering what the troops in B Company were doing at that moment.

*Are they still up in the mountains near Laos? Has supply*

*moved up there?*

Months later, I was offered a reporting job at a newspaper in Northern California. I had second thoughts about moving to the West Coast, primarily because so many of my friends from college had gone there after graduation.

I didn't want to follow the crowd, but newspaper salaries were far better in California than other places in the West. The winters were also much warmer than Montana, and the excitement of working on a daily newspaper would remain.

After accepting the newspaper job and moving to California, I still kept my thoughts of Vietnam mostly to myself. I had long since learned that it was best for veterans to be as anonymous and unspoken as possible. The only time my anonymity disappeared was when I met another Vietnam veteran.

"I hear you were in Vietnam," a newly hired reporter told me as he approached my desk in the newsroom. He was young like me, his brown hair cut short and his face deeply tanned. I had been told he was also a Vietnam veteran.

"Yeah, I was a supply sergeant for an infantry company in Quang Ngai province," I said. "What about you?"

"Just got out three weeks ago," he said. "I was an infantryman down south in the Iron Triangle near Saigon."

"Bad shit down there," I said.

"It wasn't much better up where you were," he said.

"When I first saw you, I was wondering if you were a veteran," I said.

"Why?" he asked.

"You've still got a Vietnam tan on your face."

"Oh, fuck, I'd better get rid of that," he said.

We both laughed. It always felt good to talk to another Vietnam veteran. We were the only ones who understood what we'd been through in Vietnam and what we now faced in America. If someone approached when we were talking about Vietnam, we would lower our voices or quickly change the subject.

Two weeks later, I was taking my lunch break in the newspaper cafeteria. A middle-aged woman with long brown hair approached my table.

"Do you mind if I sit down?" she asked, brushing her hair from the side of her face.

"No, go ahead." I smiled at her, but she didn't smile back.

"I hear you're a Vietnam veteran, so I wanted to give you something." She sat in the chair opposite me and reached into her purse, pulling out a small book and laying it on the table in front of me.

"It's everything you ever wanted to know about Vietnamese culture and society," she said. Her face was somber and condescending. "Maybe this book will help you understand why US forces shouldn't be in Vietnam."

I sat frozen, staring across the table at her. The fork in my right hand fell, clanking on the table.

"You're telling me I should read your book so that I'll know what Vietnam is like?" I asked.

The women's face was filled with contempt as she stared at me, nodding her head.

I grabbed the book, glanced at the cover, and flung it across the cafeteria. It landed on a nearby counter top, slid across the surface, and fell to the floor.

"You're telling me I need to read your book to know what Vietnam is like? Where the fuck do you think I've been for the past nine months!"

"You're very rude," she said as she stood to leave. "And it figures."

"I guess you've got all us Vietnam veterans figured out, haven't you?" I said. "But you don't know shit about Vietnam, and you don't know shit about what we went through over there!"

I stood and began walking out of the cafeteria, my face burning hot, my temper flaring. As I passed an empty table, I felt like grabbing it and overturning it. But I continued walking out the door and down a hallway to a side entrance to the building. I walked outside and lit a cigarette, blowing smoke back toward the building.

The next day, shortly after I arrived for work, I was

summoned into the managing editor's office. "It's okay to argue with someone," he said. "But we don't want people throwing things across the cafeteria. Someone could get hurt."

He wasn't angry when he spoke—at least, his face didn't look angry. He didn't look condescending either.

"I'm sorry," I said. "It won't happen again."

We stood and shook hands, and I turned to leave.

"What was it really like over there?" he asked.

His question surprised me, and I turned to face him. He looked like he was simply asking a question, not preparing to lecture me.

"It was bad from beginning to end—really bad," I said.

He nodded as though he understood, and I walked out of his office.

Two weeks later, a young man with shoulder-length hair approached my desk. "I heard you were in Vietnam," he said.

"Yes, I got out a year ago," I said.

"I would never go to Vietnam," he said. He spoke with a smug voice, and he wrinkled his nose as he talked to me.

I could feel my body tighten, but this time, I was determined to keep my composure. "So how did you manage to avoid going into the service?" I asked.

"I have a medical exemption."

"Well, I thought maybe your daddy knew someone on the draft board," I said, my voice suddenly sounding sarcastic.

He seemed surprised by my comment and stared at me. Then I noticed his nose; it was starting to wrinkle again.

"It's easy for you to stand there and say you would never ever go to Vietnam, but you were never drafted!" I shouted. "I was drafted. I had no choice. What the fuck was I supposed to do?"

He turned and walked away from my desk. I glanced around the newsroom; everyone was staring at me. I stood and walked out to the office, down the hallway, and out of the building to smoke a cigarette.

*This shit is really getting old*, I thought. *All I want to do is put this fucking war behind me, but these assholes won't let me.*

In the weeks that followed, I was beginning to feel detached from my surroundings. The United States was beginning to feel like a strange, almost hostile place. In Vietnam, we referred to the United States as "the world" because it seemed so distant, a world apart from Vietnam. Now that I was home, America still seemed distant, a place I had yet to reach.

Adding to my feelings of isolation and frustration, it seemed as though most Americans knew little about what was really happening in Vietnam. But they still had their opinions.

For Americans who supported the Vietnam War, there were posters outside movie theaters of John Wayne, who was starring in *The Green Berets*. John Wayne had that hard, determined look on his face that said he knew how to fight. He knew how to win a war.

For Americans against the war, there were numerous antiwar demonstrations and news photos of Jane Fonda smiling as she sat wearing a helmet in an antiaircraft battery in Hanoi.

For Americans who had grown tired of the war and its grim statistics, there was Bob Hope to cheer them up. The comedian was reaching hero status for his annual Christmas show, which he took to the troops in Vietnam. Bob Hope made Americans laugh, even while he stood telling jokes in a place where the killing never stopped.

Everything in America seemed perfectly packaged by Hollywood celebrities and television news crews. There was something for everyone, no matter what they thought of the war. But few of the images made any sense to me.

Meanwhile, the negative comments kept coming. One month later, I was at a newsman's retirement party, talking to a young man whose father piloted an army reconnaissance plane in Vietnam. The plane was shot down, and his father was badly wounded. He was evacuated from Vietnam and transported to a Veterans Administration Hospital in Seattle, where he died two months later.

"When were you in Vietnam?" the young man asked.

*Alan Quale*

"A year ago," I said.

"That's when my dad's plane was shot down," he said. "That must have really been a bad time. There were lots of wounded men from Vietnam arriving at the VA hospital where my dad was being treated."

"Yes, it was bad," I agreed. "Especially during the Tet Offensive. For a while, I thought we'd lost the war."

An older man was standing nearby, apparently eavesdropping on our conversation. He stepped forward, and paused in front of me.

"You did lose the war," he said. Then he turned and walked away.

*11 January 1969*
*Duc Pho*

*Dear Alan,*

*Greetings from Vietnam! Glad to hear you're enjoying civilian life and working in journalism. I expect nothing but the Chicago Tribune or New York Times next!*

*It's probably been a while since you heard from anyone in B Company so I thought I'd fill you in on what's been happening over here.  First, they moved the company down from up north, and they're back to patrolling the area near Pinkville. Bad news!*

*Here's a rundown on the personnel at this time. We have a new, a gung ho company commander. This is his third Vietnam tour so you can understand what it's like dealing with him. I'm still here as the company clerk (with 79 days left in Vietnam). Walsh took over as supply sergeant.*

*We had a couple of tragedies over the Christmas holidays. First, some guys were driving the jeep to a firebase near Duc Pho on Christmas Day when they were ambushed by North Vietnamese Regulars. The driver, Rodney Greenberg, was shot and killed with a bullet to the head. Greenberg only had 15 days to go in Vietnam. There was supposed to be a Christmas ceasefire! Some truce! Sanders, who was a passenger in the jeep was creased in the head with a bullet and is now back in the world, being*

245

treated at a VA hospital. Culbertson and Raymond were also in the jeep but they were only shook up.

The latest tragedy occurred on New Years Day involving Reynolds (from 3rd Platoon). He was just promoted to sergeant a month ago, but I guess the whole war situation got to him. He took his own life by placing his M16 into his mouth and pulling the trigger. We all just couldn't believe he did that.

Well, so much for the grief from this ugly, stupid war. Our only hope is to keep pushing those peace talks in Paris.

Say hi to any B Company civilians you hear from, and write again if you get the chance.


As ever,

Brad

# Chapter 15

# Dreaming of War

The dreams were always the same: I was sitting on a hard wooden seat in a dilapidated passenger car of the Vietnamese national railway. The walls were painted a faded yellow, and many of the windows were permanently stuck in the open position. A continuous breeze flowed through the car as the train rumbled down the tracks.

Looking out the window, the rice paddies slowly passed by, and in the distance, the dark-green mountains rose up, with white clouds resting on the peaks.

The train carried Vietnamese civilians and American soldiers. Cages filled with ducks and chickens were stacked at the front of the car. As the train neared a village, it slowly stopped, dropping off passengers, while others climbed on board.

I was sitting at the rear of the car and could see almost everyone. The train continued down the tracks, stopping at villages, discharging passengers and picking up others. After several stops, I noticed there were fewer American soldiers on board, but I thought nothing of it.

*There'll probably be more Americans boarding at the next station.*

The countryside passed by, and the train suddenly lurched to a stop. I assumed we had arrived at another village, but when I looked out the window, there was no station, no village—only rice fields and the distant mountains.

I turned to look at the passengers. The American soldiers were all gone. There were only Vietnamese, and they all looked angry. The Vietnamese slowly rose from their seats and begin moving toward me.

I could see the hatred in their eyes. Someone shouted in Vietnamese "slit your throat," as they pressed closer.

I rose from my seat and aimed my M16 at the crowd, but they continued moving forward. I knew it was hopeless; there were not enough bullets to stop them. The mob moved closer.

At that moment in the dream, I always awakened screaming, my arms swinging and legs kicking. My body drenched with sweat, saturated the bedsheets.

I'd get out of bed and go into the bathroom and dry myself with a towel. Then I'd light a cigarette and sit quietly in a chair, blowing smoke up toward the ceiling. Sometimes I just sat in a chair, staring at the walls.

The same nightmare continued several nights each week. At first it seemed like a nuisance that would soon go away, just another distraction facing a veteran when he returned home. But my nightmares weren't going anywhere, and they continued with regularity. The dreams were real — so real I could taste the salty air in the train car. So real I felt terror like I had never felt it before, knowing I was about to die. Each night when I climbed into bed, there was the nagging thought: *Will it happen again?*

I began to almost dread the night, just as I had in Vietnam. As my nightmares continued, everything felt hopeless, just as hopeless as everything felt in Vietnam. A strange, unsettling familiarity was settling over me.

I didn't know what to do, but I believed that if I could find the reason behind my nightmares, maybe they would go away. But as I sat chain-smoking cigarettes in the middle of the night, I couldn't find the answer. I didn't even know what I was looking for.

Months passed by. The nightmares continued, and I was nowhere near to finding an answer. All I could do was get out of bed, dry myself with a towel, and blow cigarette smoke into the air. I admitted to myself that I might never find an answer.

Adding to my confusion, my nightmares seemed real, but they were not based on fact. The Vietnamese national railway did not operate in Duc Pho when I was there. The railway tracks had long since been torn apart by mortar and artillery, and the railroad bridges were all destroyed. The train had not operated in Duc Pho for several years.

I remember the first time I saw the rail embankment

near Duc Pho. As I stood looking down the empty bank, it was almost a comical sight, with the metal tracks and crossbars bent into permanent curly cues after being struck by artillery.

But now that I had left Vietnam, there was nothing comical about my dreams. In my dreams, the Vietnamese national railway was still operating, and it was transporting me to certain death. When I awakened screaming as the mob pressed closer, it didn't matter; the train would soon return to pick me up again, and the angry mob would still be waiting.

I never told anyone about my nightmares, but when I met my future wife it became impossible to keep my nightmares secret any longer.

After one particularly bad nightmare, I woke up screaming and thrashing in bed, my body covered in sweat. We both sat up.

"What's going on?" she asked.

"I had a bad dream," I said, wiping my face with a towel.

"You've been having lots of them."

"Yeah, it's the same one."

"Is it about Vietnam?" she asked.

"Yes."

"Why don't you tell me about it?"

I took a deep breath, picked up a cigarette and lit it.

Then I began describing the nightmare — every little detail from the beginning to the end. When I finished, we both lay back down and went to sleep. I never had the nightmare again.

Psychiatrists might have a name for this sort of therapy. But I didn't care about any of that. All I knew was that my nightmares felt real, and they made my life fairly miserable until my wife rescued me by saying, "Why don't you tell me about it?" It all seemed so simple.

Still, as the years passed by, I often wondered what my subconscious was trying to tell me. There must have been some reason for having the same nightmare over and over. Now, I found the answer. I found it through the therapy of writing this book.

In my dream, the American soldiers boarding the train were replacing soldiers who were leaving. The train continued down the tracks, stopping at villages where more soldiers left and were replaced by others climbing aboard. Eventually, every soldier in the car was a replacement except for me.

Then the replacements began to leave, and soon I was the only soldier left. Suddenly I stood alone, my back against the wall and my M16 in the firing position, knowing the end was near.

My nightmare had a hidden message: I survived Vietnam, but so many others did not. My nightmare shamed me and scolded me over and over again, and then it made me feel the last terrifying moments of life itself, a feeling likely experienced by several men in B Company when they were badly wounded.

I found the meaning behind my nightmare, but the reality of my Vietnam experience is still hard for me to accept, even today. I survived mortar attacks, a booby-trapped grenade, Viet Cong assaults on my bunker, and a search for a deadly snake in the brush. I even survived being AWOL on another continent when I should have returned to Vietnam.

The stars were definitely lined up in my favor, but my fate also involved good luck, an occasional lie, and my supply sergeant job of outfitting replacements and sending them to the field while I stayed mostly in base camp. Survivor guilt can be a heavy burden, and I have my share to carry for the rest of my life.

Finally, when I look back at Vietnam, I often think of my first days in country, when I met Sergeant Sanders. I'll never forget our trip to the Catholic orphanage in Duc Pho, when I saw the young orphans in their tattered clothes selling marijuana at the gate. It was hard to believe what I was seeing, but Sergeant Sanders had an explanation:

"In Vietnam, you survive any way you can," he said. "Believe me, you'll learn that soon enough."

Made in the USA
San Bernardino, CA
10 April 2017